# Deceived

## Part 1 – New York

Eve Carter

*To my lovely family. You are everything to me.*

~\*~

# CONTENTS
~*~

Prologue       1

Chapter 1      3

Chapter 2      9

Chapter 3      21

Chapter 4      32

Chapter 5      43

Chapter 6      56

Chapter 7      63

Chapter 8      85

Chapter 9      102

Chapter 10     107

Chapter 11     113

Acknowledgments

About the Author

# PROLOGUE

**As I stood barefoot** at the water's edge, I barely noticed the freezing cold water lapping at my legs. My shoes were left behind in the loose sand. I had managed to remove them, despite my hazy state, before embarking into the Atlantic ocean on this chilly June evening. The dress would be ruined though, but I couldn't care less. Nothing really mattered much anymore.

Staring at the dark blue velvet sky over the horizon, I furiously blinked back tears of frustration, in an effort to arrest any further erosion of my soul. Every perception I had believed and trusted had changed in a split second. Paradise had been shattered into hell, desire turned into disinclination and love into hatred. Divine heavenly pleasure was now replaced by a dark excruciating pain, a pain so strong it could only be eased by walking farther and farther into the black ocean. Surely, the cold water would clear my mind, release the suffering and ache, making it all go away.

I had been deceived. Played like a dumb fool in this

billionaire's playground. I had taken part in a sensual, erotic and passionate ride that was now just an illusion, except this was not a fairytale. This was a real story and it all began a couple of weeks ago.....

# CHAPTER 1

"Miss Swanson, bring me the file for Baroness Von Lamberg". The sudden outburst from the intercom jolted me from my work-a-day concentration. I quickly gathered my wits about me and pressed down the button to answer, "Yes Sir, I will be right there with it".

Opening the file cabinet, I deftly located it under L for Lamberg and grabbing the file, I headed down the mahogany covered hallway to the office of Patrick Collins, the Agency Account Director of Meyer and Meyer.

*I can't believe it has been six months already, since I started working at the third largest ad agency in New York City.* I was so fortunate to get this assistant job, even if it is just an entry level position. For once in my life luck was on my side and I landed the job right after graduating with an MBA in Marketing from Iowa State University.

Back in college, I would lie awake at nights just dreaming about living in a big city like New York. The constant busy pulsing from the myriad of city traffic calms me and excites me at the same time. Maybe city life excites me because it's the exact opposite from my dreary life growing up in Fairfield, Iowa. Or, maybe it appeals to my hidden alter ego, a slightly darker facet of my psyche, which I like to think of, not as bad or evil, just as... a little edgy.

Arriving in front of Patrick Collins' office, I stop for a brief moment to straighten my skirt and knock on the door.

"Come in," he ordered. His deep voice from behind the door compelled me to enter.

"Here's the Baroness' file that you requested, Mr. Collins," I announced as I placed the file on his desk. I noticed how his steel-blue eyes were scanning my body, up and down its length. Subconsciously, I glanced down at my cleavage, wondering if I had opened my favorite black sweater a little too much for professional office attire, wondering if the sparkle of the open rhinestone button, that lay glistening on the roundness of my upper breast, was too enticing for my boss, Mr. Collins. Maybe it was, but I liked that thought...

"Thank you Miss Swanson. Will you close the door and sit down for a minute?" he suggested.

Nervously, I shut the door behind me and pulled out a chair.

"Have you ever heard of Baroness Anna Von Lamberg?" he inquired.

For some unexplainable reason my throat suddenly

felt as dry as a dessert storm. I tried to answer confidently, but his intense stare left me feeling slightly anxious and the words came out with a crackle.

"No Sir, I can't say I have," I replied.

"Well, she is an eccentric billionaire, controlling over twenty-five office and retail buildings in Manhattan, not to mention her inheritance of one of the largest mansions in the Hamptons. She has been a client of ours for almost ten years now, but unfortunately only regarding her charities. What we would really like, is to represent her billion dollar retail empire but so far it's been a complete dead end. You see, she can be a little - peculiar- and quite discerning at times which makes representing her almost impossible. What we need are some fresh young ideas to show her that we are a cutting edge company. And that's where your talents come in. The Baroness will be here this afternoon for a creative meeting and I would really like it if you could attend," he explained.

"Me? I mean- sure, that would be amazing!" I stuttered with surprise as I came to attention and sat up a little on the edge of my chair.

"Great!!" Patrick chimed out; satisfaction bellowing out of his voice. "I'll see you later then. The meeting is at four o'clock in the main conference room."

I took his cue as he arose from behind the dark mahogany desk, a duplicitous smile creasing his lips, and jumped to my feet. "Thank you Mr. Collins, thank you!"

Inside my head I was doing the "happy dance". I couldn't believe I got the chance to show off my ideas. My heart was racing. I imagined that I was already at the meeting delivering a marvelous oratory that astounded the entire group. I turned to make a quick exit out the door before he had the chance to change his mind when his words stopped me just shy of the threshold.

"Oh, by the way..." he interjected.

I froze in my tracks. *Oh no, - here it comes, the usual request, "Go get me some coffee..."*

"Could you do me a huge favor Miss Swanson? My niece is turning twenty-one next weekend and I need to get her a present. Would you mind picking out something for her?"

"No, not at all! What is she into...? I mean, what does she like?" I stammered. Halfway out the door, I leaned my upper body back into his office, holding the door open with one hand, gripping the door frame with the other.

"Get her an elegant dress she can wear to the Hamptons charity ball that she will be attending with me in two weeks," he said decidedly.

"Sounds great, what size is she?" I asked, while walking back into the office getting out my little notepad.

His eyes once again beamed up and down my body, this time making a, not so subtle, pause at my cleavage. "About your size I would say, except not as voluptuous up here," he said cunningly with a gesture of his hands as if he were palming two large melons. "That should do. Here, take my card," he urged.

He stood up and leaned his well-built upper body across the desk, his platinum credit card extended towards me in the fingertips of his strong hand, those steel-gray eyes piercing the air between us.

"Get something - well - that even you would wear to an A-list party," he said with a suggestive glimmer in his eyes, while handing me his credit card.

"Will do, Mr. Collins."

Something in the smile, something in his gaze made me feel aroused and weak in the knees at the same time. No sooner had the emotion washed over my body when it dissipated and I snapped out of it. No time for daydreaming now. Today is my chance to show him and the company what I'm made of, and besides, shopping for an expensive designer dress is fun, even if it's not for me.

Without another word, I quickly accepted his bid and bolted for the door, my mind whirling with a multitude of thoughts that ran the gamut from one extreme to the other. Thoughts, on the one hand of projecting a professional business woman image in the meeting, to thoughts of seductively seducing Mr. Collins on the top of the main conference room table in a tight fitting red dress, slit all the way up the side to Shangri-La.

"Oh, and be sure to be back in time to prepare for the meeting," he said coolly, as the door closed behind me with a soft whoosh and a click.

# CHAPTER 2

Rushing down the busy sidewalks of Manhattan towards Barney's Department store, I kept thinking about my big opportunity to finally show my boss that I am more than just a secretary. I couldn't quite wrap my mind around it though. Why does he really want me in the meeting? *Ha! He has finally noticed how exceptionally talented I am!* I wavered. *Yea right, Chloe.* Something doesn't add up. Sure, me being young and fitting the targeted group of people we are looking to market towards, makes me qualified, but it all sounded too good to be true. What is he up to I wondered.

My mind drifted back to the first time I met Patrick Collins six months ago. During the initial interview we exchanged handshakes and I felt a salacious propulsive energy flood my body like a deluge. I literally could have jumped his bones right then and there. I even wondered for a moment if I would be able to keep my panties dry during work! I burst out in a giggle at the absurd image of me walking through the office that way.

He certainly is a very attractive man; rugged looking, with deep set, steel-blue eyes, a solid square jaw, tobacco brown hair, and strong, wide shoulders. He had an innately captivating presence and he was *devastatingly* handsome.

*Damn*! *I wouldn't kick him out of my bed for eating crackers in it!*

At any given moment, virility emanates from his body. He exudes a sexy, hot, yet commanding aura normally associated with classic movie stars. Yes, Patrick Collins was a man's man, yet a man of contradictions. His steel-blue eyes could be cold and mysterious one moment and hold a gentle and exciting depth in another moment. He clearly works out and stays in good shape.

*Ohmigod! He's just plain hot! And he wants my input at the meeting! Woohoo! Happy dance, happy dance.*

Lost in my lusty fantasy, I almost tripped over a crack in the pavement as I thrust my shoulder into the revolving glass doors of Barney's. My mind shifted into overdrive. I only had an hour for lunch and a tall order to fill for my own Mr. Wonderful. I didn't want to let him down. The thought of disappointing him twisted in my stomach. I wanted to please him. Please him in more than one way.

~*~

I was relieved to find that the store wasn't very busy and made a beeline to the designer dresses. I knew the floor plan of Barney's like the back of my hand. If this store were a mouse maze I would have found the cheese before the buzzer sounded!

After the tortuously slow sales assistant shepherded me in and out of the fitting rooms with six different dresses, I finally found the perfect one. It was a floor length, sleeveless, black crepe, Prabal Gurung designer gown, with a ruched, V-neck, draped bodice. It was gorgeous! It was elegant. It was $3000!

*Hope he really loves his niece!*

Tick, tock, time was running out. I nailed the elevator button with the point of my elbow as my lunch hour screeched to an end. I bolted out of the elevator door on the 26th floor of the Seagram building, where Meyer and Meyer housed their lavish offices, my arms draped with a Barney's garment bag. A fashionable shoe bag hung from the crux of my elbow, a cell phone rested in my one hand, while I sucked on an ice cold Starbuck's Frappuccino cupped in the other hand.

Looking like a juggling act for a three-ring-circus, I went crashing down the hall to my office. No sooner had I rounded the corner when my new favorite best friend, Elyse, just about knocked me over like a bowling pin. My drink cup slammed up against my chest, almost ripping off the lid. Images of coffee stains dribbled down the front of a *freaking-$3000* dress jack knifed the word out of my mouth, "*Shit!*"

"Sorry honey! Are you okay? Did I spill your coffee on you? What's the big hurry anyway?" she implored.

"You wouldn't believe it, Elyse!" I said with a huff.

She followed me to my desk, in her baby-step fashion, an awkward gate induced by heels that were too high for office attire. Taking the coffee cup out of my hand, she proceeded to unload my arms of each item, one by one. Arms free of my shopping burden, I ushered her around behind the desk away from prying ears and excitedly explained in a low voice.

"Listen to this," I breathed excitedly as I picked up the nearest notebook and stood poised with a pen in my hand, so if anyone was looking they would think we were discussing business.

"Mr. Collins called me into his office this morning and told me to shut the door and sit down. I had no idea what was up because he never does that. Jeez, he's so hot and I was sweating bullets just staring at his strong square jaw while the words rolled out of his mouth. It was like one of those movie scenes where the leading lady sees the mouth moving but can't hear the words because she is so enamored by the guy."

"Alright already!" Elyse said impatiently, "I get it. He's a hunk. Yada, yada, yada, just get to the point girl!"

I broke out of my false business-conversation pose and put my props down on the desk, too consumed with excitement to pretend I was calmly working. Leaning into each other, Elyse and I sat down at the same time in chairs behind my desk.

"Today, at four o'clock, there is a meeting with one of the company's most prestigious clients, Baroness Von Lamberg. Mr. Collins wants fresh cutting edge ideas to present and asked me to attend." The words spilled out of my mouth like water over a broken levy.

"No way! That's fantastic. Stepping up to the big league now," she confirmed.

"I know," I nodded, "but get this, then he whips out his credit card and waves it in my face saying he wants me to buy a birthday gift for his niece."

"Well, that's not so weird. Lots of bosses ask their office girls to run errands," she affirmed.

"I know, but it was more in the way he asked and the tone in his voice."

"Oh, he has the hots for you Chloe!" Elyse smiled teasingly.

"Stop it!" I objected. "He's my boss. Maybe I'm just reading too much into this thing. He could have any woman, hell, he could have a whole harem of hot, sexy young women, with big tits and tight round asses from here to eternity. I don't stand a chance. I'm sure this is just another one of my "delusions of grandeur"."

"What - are you saying that you are schizo or something?" she joked.

"Ha! No, this guy just drives me crazy. Elyse, the way he looked at me across the desk today was so intense. All I wanted was to straddle him over the desk and shove my tongue down his throat, until the people a floor below could hear the desk thumping!" I rocked back in laughter at the thought of the two of us going at it on his desk.

"When he was checking me out, he did that guy thing where his eyes were talking to my tits."

"And what did your "tits" say back to him?" she said with a smirk.

I snorted a little laugh.

"I don't know. I'm sure it's all in my imagination anyway."

"Chloe, listen to me, you are a hottie. Of course he's interested. He'd have to be dead from the waist down not to notice how beautiful you are. Your sweetheart shaped face is every guy's dream; you have long legs that always look amazing in heels, and the fact that you have to shop in the double D drawer at Victoria's Secret, makes you the envy of every girl."

"I can always count on you to build me up Elyse. Thanks buttercup." Elyse rolled her eyes and groaned at my stupid joke.

I sighed and leaned my elbow on my desk. A pile of paperwork shifted in response to my motion and white copy paper fluttered to the floor like the wings of a dove. The noise jerked my attention to the clock.

*Crap!* I needed to prepare for the meeting and it was

only a few hours away, but first I had a more pressing matter at hand.

Quickly I scooped up the dress, intent on delivering the treasure to Patrick. I hoped that, when he saw the dress for his niece, he would be dazzled with my fashion acuity. I prickled with delight at the thought of how his face would light up when I showed him the gown. I carried it like a jewel on a pillow to his office.

He was on the phone when I peeked my head in. I pushed the door open a little with my foot, the garment bag draped over both my outstretched arms like I was presenting him with a cake.

I could see that he was in the middle of a call, but he waved me in from behind his desk and hung up the phone.

"Come in, come in, Chloe," he urged. He moved out from behind the desk to meet me, gently taking the garment bag from my arms. "This is great Chloe! I can't wait to see the dress. I'm sure you have exquisite taste." He started to reach for the zipper but stopped.

"Wait. Would you, would you- um -show me by trying it on?" he suggested.

I tilted my head a little to one side and gave him a *"What the hell?"* look and instinctively took a step back.

He laid the bag out on the length of his office couch and walked towards me with those beautiful sexy eyes beaming straight into my soul.

Face to face, he gently took hold of my arms in his

15

strong hands, halting my escape with a firm grip. I could feel the heat from his body radiating into my personal perimeter and then straight into my inner being, where the mixture of the smell of his cologne and charm melted my heart.

I knew that I shouldn't have these forbidden feelings, but my mind was swimming through a haze of emotions and desire. My breathing picked up, and I felt a warm tingling feeling pulsate through my body from head to toe. I was almost sure that under his fingers, he must have felt the buzzing of my sentient pleasure. He was my boss. But I didn't care. In this moment in time we were the only two people in the universe.

He held me at arm's length and I felt the slightest pull of his fingertips on my arms, as if to suggest that he wanted to pull me into an embrace, but he faltered in the silence that engulfed us. We stood there, locked into each other's gaze, frozen in time. I burned with passion for him, longing for his lips to find mine in a reverie of wet, hot kisses.

His expression was hungry and lustful but I didn't want to put him in a compromising position. In today's business place no one wants to face the possibility of getting slapped with a sexual harassment lawsuit. I wanted to melt into his arms but instead I desperately tried to take control of my emotions and change the direction of where things were going; the pace of my breathing causing my speech to falter a little.

"Well, Mr. Collins, I, ah... well... I suppose I could.

Do you want me to take it down to the restroom and try it?" I was turning into a pile of melted butter under his riveting stare.

The buzzer suddenly squawked on his intercom breaking his gaze. He turned reluctantly to answer the intercom, "Not now Clare," he said impatiently and turned back to me.

"No, not the ladies room." He looked around the room and took a few steps toward the back office.

"How about in here? Yea, here. Come back here to my file room. I was going to keep the dress here anyway until her birthday."

He picked up the garment bag and led the way back to his little annex where he kept his confidential files. I could see the warm yellow light of a lawyer's lamp sitting on a small mahogany writing desk, softly shining out of the room, balancing out the harsh fluorescent lights of the hallway. It was a small room with no windows; the walls were lined with bookshelves, file cabinets and a coat rack where he hung his stylish overcoat, stood just inside the door.

"In here?" I asked with some trepidation. I scanned the room as we walked inside but decided it would do. It was better than trying to put on a $3000 designer dress in the stall of the ladies' washroom.

"Okay. Just give me a minute."

He delicately hung the dress in the garment bag on the coat rack, and carefully smoothed out the bottom of the bag so it wouldn't crumple. I loved the way he paid attention to details of the things he cared about.

"There you go beautiful," he winked. "Knock yourself out. I'll be right outside the door."

Once the door closed, I kicked off my high heels and shoved them to the side of one of the file cabinets. In one fell swoop my work clothes dropped to the floor with a soft swoosh. I carefully unzipped the garment bag painfully aware of the time constraints. The conference was fast approaching, but my ardent desire to please Patrick, pushed aside any thoughts of the four o'clock meeting and I quickly slipped on the long flowing gown. I gingerly opened the door a crack. I didn't know whether to walk out to show him or wait for him to come in, but decided to just let the door swing open and stood there at the threshold.

"Voila!" I said with a gesture like I was the magician's assistant who had just reappeared after a vanishing act.

Patrick had been waiting just outside the door texting on his cell phone. When he heard the door open he spun around to look. He sucked in a short breath and said, "Wow Chloe! You're so beautiful! You look stunning in that dress!"

Pleased with his reaction, I turned around in a little circle so he could get a 360 degree view. "Oh, sorry, I couldn't quite reach to finish zipping up the back. Could you help me get the zipper?" I asked as I pulled my long hair to one side and exposed my back to him. I waited in that pose holding my hair aside and my neck elongated. I anticipated the pressure of his hand on the zipper but instead I felt the steam of his breath on the back of my neck. I inhaled the toxic ardor of his cologne and with his hand he smoothed my hair aside to expose even more of the back of my neck. I made no effort to retreat. I closed my eyes and drank in the erotic surge of energy that was transferred from his body to mine, only nanoseconds away from me. Currents of desire pulsed through my nervous system and rocked the stability of my very soul. His presence unleashed in me an impulsive fire that I had never felt before. I wanted to fall into his arms and give myself to him with liberated passion.

His warm, soft, lips touched the surface of my neck and he slowly and seductively began kissing my bare skin, sending a crescendo of sensual nerve signals to flood my brain. The combination of his fervent kisses on my neck and his hard body pressing up against my back, made an amalgam like soup of my thoughts. A tornado of sexual feelings turned into a mind boggling dizziness that left me weak in the knees. All logic and reason flew out the window and I longed to give in to his hypnotic force. My pulse quickened in an instant and the force of the air pulling at my lung, compelled me to open my mouth as if to pant for more of his energy.

Breathlessly, he whispered my name, licking on the lobe of my ear, running his tongue around its edges, and gently teasing the lobe between his teeth. With one last long gentle suck he released it and he spoke in a broken whisper, "Chloe, I ….." his words strangled by his emotions.

I released a slight moan as he cupped my face in his hand to turn my lips towards his. The heat of the moment melted the words in my throat into a whimpering surrender and his lips crushed down on mine in a fiery cascade of hot, wet kisses that were met with complete abandon. He pulled me in hard to his chest, ravaging my mouth with his tongue, one arm encircling my body while the other hand pushed and squeezed at my breast. The dress had fallen off one shoulder, and his grasping hand had worked the fabric down to expose the creamy upper crest of my heaving breast.

"Mr. Collins, Baroness Von Lamberg is on her way for the 4:00 meeting," I heard Clare's shrill voice shriek out over the intercom.

"Damn technology! Always intruding when you least want it," Patrick growled annoyed.

Opening my eyes I came back to reality and an eternal ache was sparked by that one indelible kiss..

# CHAPTER 3

My heart was beating with excitement as I prepared the conference room for the meeting. Finally, I get a chance to show everybody that I am more than just a secretary. At last, a chance to use my degree for something more than simply knowing how many pieces of sugar everyone takes in their coffee. As I laid out copies of the proposal that Patrick had prepared, he swiftly entered the room.

"Chloe, Let me give you a quick briefing before the Baroness comes in," he explained. "This is just the proposal for promoting her charity; however, the real goal today is to find an opportunity for a discussion about representing her billion dollar retail empire. Remember, as I told you earlier, she can be a little strange and quite demanding, so this will not be a walk in the park, but we really need this account-- no matter what it takes."

Leaning in, he whispered into my ear, "Even if we have to seduce her!"

A quiver dissipated throughout my body as he

entered my space. I could feel the warmth of his breath on my face. For a brief moment, I closed my eyes to breath in the essence that was his and the memory of our passionate kiss came flooding back into my mind at warp speed. I fought the urge to keep my eyes closed and drink in the musky scent of his cologne, longing to feel his skin against my face. With a little flutter of my eyelashes, I forced myself to open my eyes and snap out of it.

"S-seduce her?" I stammered dizzily.

He pulled back from me with a little chuckle in his voice, "Yeah. "

Obviously he was teasing me, but he had found the weak chink in my armor. One step into my personal space and I was putty in his hands. He moved around to the back of his desk, dropped down in his chair and leaned back leisurely.

"I know she is impressed with our work here at Meyer and Meyer, and all she needs is a little push to come over to our side for the retail account," he said with his boyish smile. "But I really need your help Chloe. We have to present a young fresh image and today we have one shot to get her attention for the big account, however, I think we need to get her alone. That won't happen here, because she will be bringing her lawyer and assistant with her. She never takes meetings without them. There's no way we can dazzle her with those moron goons around."

"I-I'd love to help but how?" I said a little baffled.

"Don't look so startled, honey", he laughed gently.

"It's all just a good innocent game of seductive business. I know exactly what to do, so let me take care of the details. Just follow my lead, okay?"

I blinked in bewilderment. "Anything you say, Boss," I spouted with mock servitude.

At exactly four o'clock the Baroness entered the conference room like a queen with her two escorts. She swooped in, flanked on her right by the personal assistant and on her left by the lawyer. The assistant was a tall, good looking young man with a slender build. He had a porcelain complexion on chiseled features, set against dark auburn hair, which was swept up with a handful of hair gel, into a modern cosmopolitan hairstyle. I thought it was interesting that the Baroness would not have a female assistant. *Humph.* Probably doesn't like competing for looks with a younger woman. The lawyer was a very short round Italian-looking, little man, dressed impeccably well. He looked like a younger Danny DeVito in an Armani suit.

After the entourage was seated, I looked over the Baroness in greater detail. She appeared to be about thirty something, but was probably more like in her early forties. She was captivating! Her long dark hair flowed loosely to her shoulders in soft curls. The fashionable way in which her hair swept back from her face, gave the impression that she was standing in a constant breeze. Her eyes were smoky, and her upper lip made the perfect heart shape of Cupid's bow. A real beauty for her age and likely intelligent too, considering all her wealth from her retail business.

*Damn!* Looks like there could be some competition for Patrick's attention here, but I couldn't be concerned with that at the moment. My mission was to dazzle everybody with my business acuity, save the day, and make Patrick eternally indebted to me.

The meeting started as any meeting would, with introductions all around the table. The minute the Baroness' assistant, Kurt, opened his mouth to speak, I knew we didn't sing from the same choir book, and the minute the Baroness opened hers, I knew she was a...... *BITCH*! She glared at me with distaste and as the meeting unfurled, her mode of communication showed that she was completely lacking an internal censor of her perceptions. I imagined that she frequently thought of herself as sensitive, but in reality she only had frankness, lacking any perceptiveness. She came across abrasive and unreasonable, except to Patrick's authority, or to whoever would benefit her in the moment.

She looked at me like I was a crumb she needed to flick off her shoe. A leftover morsel of the last poor soul she had chewed up and spit out at lunch. I knew in a New York minute that I wasn't going to like this women one bit. *Argh! This woman was getting under my skin.*

Patrick began to lay out the details of the upcoming charity campaign.

"After reviewing all the details of your campaign Anna, Chloe and I had some fresh ideas of how we can aggressively promote your charity to a wider and younger audience. "

She rotated her body in the chair to face him and spoke very distinctively. "Patrick, I have every confidence that *you* have come up with some magnificent ideas which I would love to discuss with you in further detail." The word "love" lingered on her tongue like a red hot cinnamon candy; her eyes burning holes into Patrick.

Not once had she addressed me so far during the meeting. She talked over me like I was invisible and every time Patrick asked for my opinion on a matter; a shadow of annoyance crossed her face. The Baroness directed her comments exclusively to Patrick, or her two flunkies, but never to me. I was getting steamed and looked towards Patrick for help. In a brief moment I thought I saw a couple beads of sweat forming on the edge of his hairline, but it was just my imagination and as usual he was his calm collected self, measuring her with a cool appraising look.

"So Anna, I suggest we sequester ourselves behind closed doors to go over the new ideas in details," he said.

"That's a brilliant idea. Let's talk further at dinner tonight, just you and me" she insisted.

Was she flirting with him? Worse yet, was he flirting with her? I figured Patrick was just blowing smoke. He was a pretty good actor, persuading her with his handsome face, and his steel-blue eyes. Even her assistant, Kurt, and "Danny DeVito" felt the tension rising between the two of them. Kurt pursed his lips and raised his eyebrows. The lawyer nervously shuffled his papers. I shifted restlessly in my chair, repositioning for the attack. No way was I going to back out now. Patrick was mine. This she-devil had better check her attitude at the door, because I was about to come out full barrel.

Pushing back my chair and raising to my feet I confidently began to deliver my pitch.

"Baroness Von Lamberg, please allow me to show you the marketing strategy that I have designed for your campaign that will increase your audience by at least thirty-five percent. For example last month's reach was onl....."

Before I had a chance to finish my pitch, I was abruptly interrupted by the Baroness. "Patrick, I need some real coffee, not this liquid mud you call coffee. Send your girl out to Starbucks to get me a decent cup of coffee."

"Sure, of course, whatever you want Anna...," he complied. "Chloe, please go and get some new coffee for the Baroness."

I hesitated for a split second and blinked my eyes. I couldn't believe my ears. She had my Patrick wrapped around her little finger and the direction of things was heading south. Embarrassment siphoned the blood from my face. I pursed my lips and couldn't bear to look directly at him.

"Yes, of course Mr. Collins." I said talking to the tabletop. Without saying another word I collected my papers, stood up and headed for the door.

"Darling, please make sure they use soy milk and not real milk," the Baroness said her last words spoken to the back of the glass conference room door.

Feeling demeaned and betrayed, I charged off in the direction of the elevators not even stopping at my desk. Staring straight ahead, eyes focused on the elevator door, with one hand I flung my executive binder in the near vicinity of my desk as I charged past it. Heads turned and eyebrows rose as I plowed my way down the aisles of cubicles. I had to get out of there. I needed to escape. I felt like the air was being sucked out of my lungs. A knot formed in my throat and I could feel the tears welling up in my eyes. I didn't want to give in to the emotions, the hurt and the humiliation, which would steep like a noxious tea brewing in the pit of my stomach; a brew that would later be condensed into a thick reduction sauce of anxiety that I would taste for years to come. Most of all, I just didn't want anyone to see me cry. I wanted to be a thick-skinned businesswoman but instead I felt like a scolded school child. Not only was I humiliated by the way the Baroness demeaned me; I was deeply hurt by how Patrick gave in to her demands and wouldn't stand up for me.

As an assistant, I learned quickly to accept that I

have to serve other people with a smile. I have done so for six months now and I've come to expect a little bit of everything. However, nobody prepared me for what it feels like when someone whom I trusted, admired and adored, suddenly and without warning or hesitation, pulled the rug out from under my feet. I was crushed. My heart sunk into my chest until I thought it would fall right out and hit the ground.

I had been walking in such a daze that I didn't even realize the direction in which I was heading and before I knew it, I had spun around a corner, passed the office elevators, ending right in front of the ladies restroom. I fell in the door breathing hard from trying to hold back the flood of emotions. I needed a place to hide and pull myself together. I needed Elyse to solace me. I closed my eyes feeling utterly miserable. I leaned on the countertop below the mirror with both hands, waiting for my breathing to slow down, the taste of saline seeping into the corners of my mouth. I wiped away my tears with the back of my hand and hung my head down. Taking a shaky deep breath I tipped my head back and exhaled slowly. If anyone was in the restroom with me, I didn't even care.

I caught my image in the mirror; red faced and eyes starting to puff. *Oh shit, I can't go back to the meeting looking like this.*

I blotted my face with a cool moist paper towel. The cry baby I saw in the mirror was not how I had envisioned myself in New York. As I stared at my reflection, I felt something turn inside my mind, something began to arise from the depths of my psyche. Slowly it arose, starting as a simmer, and then rumbling to a boil until determination was bursting from every pore of my being. There was no way in hell I was going to buckle under the pressure of Patrick's self-sufficing need for a high priced client and let them see how they had gotten the better of me. .

If I ever wanted a promotion or Patrick for that matter, I had better get my act together and get back there before the Baroness coerced Patrick into some fishy deal. My heart softened a little as I thought about how naive Patrick was to her witchery. I doubted that he was even aware of the slick pathos of persuasion that she was using on him. He did imply that he would do anything to get her big account, even "seduce" her. Suddenly, I felt like an idiot for getting so upset. Cleary Patrick was just playing the Baroness. *"Follow my lead"* he had even instructed me. If I was going to be a true competitive New Yorker, I had better learn not to take things so damn personally. *I was such a Dorothy.*

I gathered myself and exited the building. Ten minutes later I grabbed a coffee at the nearest Starbucks, made to perfection for even the most persnickety coffee aficionado, and headed back to the meeting with a renewed resolve. My luck not-withstanding, I arrived back at the meeting just as they were wrapping thing up. No sooner had I placed the coffee on the table when the Baroness took one sip and turned up her nose.

"It's cold" she sniffed and pushed it aside.

I wasn't even ruffled. I had anticipated as much. I sweetly smiled at her and then at Patrick with a nod. He gave me a probing look and sweeping up the coffee cup in one hand, I promptly dropped it in the trash with a punctuated thud.

With an apologetic look in his eyes Patrick said, "I'm sorry Chloe, we've just about wrapped everything up here this afternoon. If you would please, take these notes and type them up for me, I think we're about out of time here today. It's getting late and the Baroness and I should head out for the business dinner at Scalini's."

"Certainly Mr. Collins, I'll type it up for you so you will have it by tomorrow." I said calmly.

The Baroness arose from her seat, obviously having had her fill of tedious business talk for the day. She was notorious for dismissing people and true to form, she waved away her assistant and her lawyer. As she spun her gossamer around Patrick, her two assistants scurried out the door in fear of getting caught in its sticky threads. With only the three of us left in the room, the Baroness' demeanor changed toward Patrick. She was all over him like white on rice. I felt like vomiting at the seductive syrupy sweet tone in her voice, so I decided this was a good time to leave. One second longer and I may have scratched her eyes out.

"Oh, Chloe, one more thing before you go; make

reservations for the Baroness and I at Scalini's. And ask for the private side room, would you please."

*Shit! The web was spun.*

# CHAPTER 4

Back in my office, I finished typing up the notes from the meeting and walked down the dark halls to deliver them to Patrick's office. Everyone had gone home, except me, there as usual, working late. Entering his office I paused for a moment to put the papers on his desk. His chair was swiveled in my direction, as if an open invitation appeared. My fingers traced an imaginary design over the black leather of his throne. I sat down in the soft expensive leather of his chair. It smelled faintly of his cologne. As I leaned back, my thoughts triggered old emotions. The disappointment of the meeting still haunted me. I couldn't get the image of the Baroness flirting with Patrick out of my mind. Flirting was putting it mildly, she was aggressively attacking. A wave of apprehension swept through me. My mind was a crazy mixture of hope and fear. Hope, which sprang from the way Patrick had kissed me earlier and fear, which erupted from the fact that the Baroness could ruin what Patrick and I had started together.

Lost in a daydream, I couldn't help but wonder if he, at the moment of the kiss, could smell the musk of my wetness wafting up from between my thighs. His panty-dropping kiss had kept me wet for hours.

With feelings of great annoyance, I was jerked out of my reverie by the buzzing of a cellphone on the desk! I reached out my arm, exuding an audible *"Argh!"* as I snatched it up. *Shit! Patrick forgot his phone.* He must have been in such a hurry to get to the restaurant that he left his phone behind.

A mischievous plan began to take form in my mind as I sat there staring at Patrick's cell phone in my hand. I grabbed my coat and dashed out of the office.

Once on the street level, I hurriedly attempted to hail a cab.

"Taxi!!" I yelled loudly. I was impatiently hopping from foot to foot, my pulse throbbing from nervous tension. *If I'm gonna go through with this, I'd better just do it before I chicken out.*

But as usual when you really need a cab, it's almost impossible to get their attention. Finally, after what seemed like an eternity, one obliging cab driver noticed the desperate look that was plastered on my face and pulled over. I dropped down into the back seat of the cab.

"Where to Miss?" he inquired in a gruff voice.

"Scalini's at Duane Street and step on it!" I could see the raised eyebrow look of the husky cab driver in the reflection of the rearview mirror.

"Yes Ma'am!" Something cautioned him not to ask any further questions.

The traffic wasn't bad, so I took a deep breath and tried to relax to no avail, as there was a lingering tenseness in my body. I chewed on my lip nervously as the cab driver careened around corners and zigzagged his way down the streets. Fifteen minutes later he pulled up in front of Scalini's. The meter showed $11.50. I handed him three five dollar bills and jumped out of the cab.

As I stood in the front lobby of the restaurant, a wave of nausea turned my stomach into knots. I was getting cold feet. Suddenly the idea of interrupting their business dinner, just to get Patrick's attention, no longer seemed like such a great idea. But this wasn't just about getting his attention, I reminded myself, this was about blocking the Baroness' attack on Patrick. I couldn't let her stop me from my true mission. Fear and uncertainty gripped at my thoughts. My determination faltered briefly, but my resolve surfaced again when I remembered how sweet his lips had tasted when we kissed and how secure I felt in his embrace. The mere thought of the passion was more than enough to magically dissolve any doubt that had raised its ugly head. *Play to your opponent's weakness Chloe, play to her weakness!*

A gorgeous dark Italian looking host greeted me at the reservation desk.

"Good evening Miss. Welcome to Scalini Fedeli.

Could I have your name for the reservation?"

"I'm just here to meet my boss, Mr. Patrick Collins" I replied nervously.

"Oh yes! Mr. Collins..." He glanced at the seating plan. "Right this way Miss." The handsome young man swiftly guided me around the elegant main dining tables into the secluded side room.

"Chloe," Patrick exclaimed, clearly surprised. "What are you doing here?" He stood up, greeting me with one arm outstretched and the other one holding his napkin. It was obvious that I had interrupted the Baroness' ploy for Patrick's attention. Her expression was one of pained intolerance and her lips puckered with annoyance. She didn't even attempt to hide her distaste at seeing me.

"You forgot your iPhone at the office and it kept ringing, so I thought you might need it," I explained as I handed over the cellphone. A deep chill ran down my spine, as I felt eyes of steel burning into me from across the table, where the baroness was sitting.

"If my head wasn't attached I'd forget that too! Thank you so much Chloe," Patrick beamed.

"Oh, no problem. It was nothing." I said with the most seductive smile in my arsenal.

"Well, seeing that you came all the way down here let me at least offer you a drink." His eyes swept the room with a searching glance. "Tony, we need another chair here. Would you bring one for Miss Swanson?" he said with a wave of his hand.

"Certainly, Mr. Collins," Tony replied.

Perturbed with my decision to stay for a drink, the Baroness' eyes flashed me a cold glance, so I welcomed Patrick's offer and a couple of minutes later, a perfectly crafted Gray Goose vodka Cosmopolitan was sitting in front of me. Feeling a little unnerved under the Baroness' razor- sharp scrutiny, I downed half my drink in one gulp.

So far the plan had worked like a charm. I had interrupted the Baroness' attempts to steal my prince and the ball was now back in my court.

"Tell me Chloe, how long have you worked for Patrick?" the baroness asked pryingly.

"Oh - only about six months," I replied not quite sure where she was going with this.

"And you've already been promoted?" she insinuated. "You must be really good at what you do?" her tongue was heavy with sarcasm. "And what exactly is it you, *do,* so well?" The contemptuous tone in her voice angered me, but I wasn't about to let her get to me for a second time in one day. I was holding my tongue, hoping she would back off but the baroness kept going, twisting that knife even deeper.

Patrick must have sensed that an argument was about to erupt, like a steaming volcano, and before I had the chance to speak, he quickly interrupted.

"I'm considering Chloe as my new apprentice and she is showing very, very promising results." He gently laid his hand on my forearm, "In fact, I don't think it will be long before I'll have to look for a new assistant, as Chloe will be moving up in the firm."

*Touché Bitch!* My gorgeous Patrick came to my rescue with perfect timing. His admiration of me made me smile. I had never learned how to accept a compliment graciously and like an idiot, I blushed flipping my hair with my free hand in a subconsciously flirtatious gesture. The Baroness clenched her mouth tighter and flopped back in her chair with a look of resignation on her face. However, I didn't believe for a minute that she had given up and I could feel the cold between us turning to ice.

The second Gray Goose Cosmo was almost emptied and I was starting to feel the effects of the alcohol. A little voice in my head warned, "*You better slow down*", but today I wasn't listening. I was suffering from acute alcohol induced deafness! The pressure of the Baroness' interrogation strategies crushed me like a vice grip. Due to my alcoholic stupor, my temporary deafness was also coupled with blindness-to-reason. I convinced myself, as most drunks will agree, that inebriation is a sure fire method to better withstand abusive attacks from conniving bitches. So, I ordered another drink and added, "Make it a double, Tony," reeling back in my chair.

Patrick turned with a wink and gave me one of his beautiful smiles. Meanwhile the venomous vixen geared up for her next onslaught.

"Tell me, sweetie, any boyfriend back in..... where is

it you come from again?" the Baroness chided.

"Iowa. And no, I don't have a boyfriend. I'm absolutely, one hundred percent single", I said firmly while shifting my gaze towards Patrick.

"Oh yes, Iowa. "Cow country," right? That's so wonderful dear," she said placatingly. "It really suits you well. I can see so much of that "cowgirl" shape... well...cowgirl type in you. Were you husky as a child, or just a tomboy....? Well, never mind. I suppose it doesn't matter really, there's always liposuction."

My eyes widened with indignation! Well, at least they tried to widen but my "Bette Davis eyes" had now turned into "Gray Goose eyes," reduced to sleepy little slits, half closed from the effects of the alcohol. *Damn Bitch!* I struggled to keep the words from leaping out of my mouth. I wanted to launch a barrage of clever admonishments at her but instead I just forced a sarcastic smile. *Shit! I gotta pee!*

My eyes focused on Patrick with heavy desire as he chatted with the Baroness, parlaying bits of information back and forth, in between sips of their drinks. I watched his mouth forming the words and longed for those luscious lips of his to drive me wild again with delight.

The booze had really kicked in by now and I felt a little light-headed as I stood up from the table.

"Excuse me, I need to go powder my nose," I said with as much control as I could muster. Patrick, being the eternal gentleman that he was, stood up and acknowledged my exit. I floated away towards the restroom sign in the corner, distracted by thoughts of Patrick kissing me all over my body, not caring that the Baroness' evil glare was following my every move.

Moments later, I impatiently turned the lock inside one of the restroom stalls and was finally able to take a deep breath of relief, being away from the Baroness' critical interrogation. I couldn't help but think that maybe I was way in over my head here. How will I be able to compete with this worldly woman? She has everything! She is undoubtedly extremely sexy, she is beyond stinking-rich and she has something that Patrick really wants; a big fat contract.

The alcohol made me quite dizzy so I leaned up against the inside of the stall. With my back against the wall, I closed my eyes and tipped my head back, still thinking about Patrick. My pulse quickened, as I remembered the sensuousness of his skin next to mine, the way it had felt when the warmth of his lips pressed against my neck. A hot little tingle erupted in the sweet spot between my thighs. My eyes rolled back in my head a little and my hand raced down my stomach towards my crotch. With one hand clutched to my breast and the other sticking to the wetness in my panties, my imagination launched a recap of Patrick and I, back at the office in the little file room where I tried on the dress. The mere thought of taking my clothes off in his private space, catapulted yet another surge of warm wonderful tingles all the way down and I had to touch myself. The flashback of our intense kiss was making me so hot.

The area between my legs was quivering with excitement and I had to respond. I hiked up my dress, slid my hand into my lace, thong panties and gently started rubbing my finger on top of my clit. It felt delicious! I involuntarily let out a little moan. I was imagining Patrick's warm breath on my neck, his lips gently touching my skin and the soft spot between my shoulder and neck. With the panties now down my black boots, I started rubbing harder, as I imagined his warm hands fondling and squeezing tight around my voluptuous breasts and the tips of his fingers massaging my nipples.

In my fantasy, I was unzipping his pants and his hard cock was straining against his boxers; delivering a small drop of pre-cum, evidence of his lust for me. I imagined that I tore his shorts down with one hand and with a firm grip I wrapped my other hand around his enormous penis stroking it hard. I imagined his hand moving towards my bare mound, as my fingers were now running deep circles around my now engorged clit. I was now so close to exploding in a massive orgasm but a loud screeching voice abruptly interrupted me,

"Is that you in there Chloe? What are you doing?"

*Fuck!! It's the Baroness!!*

She had been standing right outside my bathroom stall and had clearly heard everything. Still feeling heady from the alcohol and the blood rush of my sexual excitement, I rolled to my left and my shoulder hit the door of the stall making the door lock clatter. I laughed a drunken laugh. *Busted!*

I rearranged my undergarment and smoothed my skirt back down. Unlocking the door I stumbled out of the stall, slurring my speech, "What's up B-Baroness? I put emphasis on the B sound and practically spat the words in her face. *Baroness Bitch! I wanted to say.* I was teetering from the drinks but somehow in my delirium, I found a renewed determination to stand up to this woman.

"Do you really think being a Baroness makes you special? "

Her eyes narrowed seething with impending anger. I could tell from her look that she wasn't used to being confronted in this manner.

"I may be from Iowa but at least I have a tight little ass, unlike your droopy old sagging butt. So take your Botox laden lips and please get out of my way?"

I attempted to brush past the Baroness to re-apply my lip gloss in the mirror, when I felt a vice-like grip on my throat. I had been spun around by her maneuver and I felt the air being pushed out of my lungs, as I was slammed up against the bathroom wall. The hard jolt sent a ringing in my ears. I felt a hand sliding up under my dress and grabbing my crotch hard, as the other hand on my throat made it nearly impossible for me to breath.

"You have absolutely no idea what you are up

against you dirty little cunt. If I were you, I'd run home, pack my bags and go back to that miserable little town I came from," she warned.

I heard a muffled rip of my lace thong, which was still soaking wet from masturbating. My peripheral vision warped into a black blur, as I felt two fingers grotesquely thrust into my vagina, and the baroness grunted into my face, "I bet that you were fantasizing about dear Patrick fucking you like this while you were masturbating in there. Keep dreaming. He's a million miles out of your league, you fucking little whore!"

A wave of nausea turned my stomach as her sour alcohol breath spewed out the words. I was nearly on the brink of losing consciousness, when the Baroness finally released her death grip on my throat; a grip born out of jealousy and hatred. Completely startled and shocked by the brutal attack, I buried my face in my hands, and slowly melted down the wall of the ladies room to the marble floor, as the Baroness exited.

# CHAPTER 5

I was crumpled on the floor inside Scalini's Ladies room, for what seemed like an eternity, though it had probably been not more than a couple of minutes, when the soft whoosh sound of air being sucked in by an open door fell on my ears. An elderly woman with white hair and wearing a soft pink dress entered the restroom.

"Oh dear God child, are you okay?" she asked while helping me to my feet. I was desperately clutching the strap of my purse in one hand and I could see in the mirror over her shoulder that my hair was all messed up. It must have happened as I slid down the wall. I felt embarrassed and a slight flush washed over my face.

"Yes, I slipped on the floor. Thank you so much for helping" I replied.

I stepped over to the mirror to fix my hair and smooth my clothes, as I pondered how I was going to get out of the restaurant without facing another encounter with the Baroness.

I took a deep breath and peaked out the door to

discern my route of escape, when I noticed that Patrick was sitting alone.

"There you are," Patrick said relieved as I approached the table. "Are you okay? You were gone for a long time," he implored his eyes searching mine for the truth.

I was still rather shaken up by the bizarre restroom incident, but by no means would I let Patrick see me defeated and weak. Instead I put on a happy smile and said, "I'm sorry Patrick. It must have been the drinks that got to my stomach. Where is the Baroness?"

"She had to leave. You do look a little unsettled," he said with concern in his voice. "Come, I'll take you home," and with a firm hand on the small of my back, he guided me towards the exit. I felt a wave of relief wash over my body, triggered by his gentle touch, as we made our way to the parking attendant. The night air had turned cold and a shiver passed over my body. Patrick instinctively pulled me into his warmth, and put a strong muscular arm around my shoulder. I succumbed to his comfort and support as we waited for the valet to bring around his car, my hands clenched in knotted fingers from the anxiety of the secret I was now hiding.

When the car finally arrived, my nerves had settled and I was feeling more like myself again. The valet regally held the passenger door open and I entered with the air of a princess.

"A Jaguar. Very nice Patrick," I said as I slid

comfortably into the sleek black leather seats.

"Oh, you know cars. That's good. I love British cars. My next car will be an Aston Martin. I've had my eye on one for a while now."

"Are you sure you can live up to driving James Bond's car?" I fondly teased. In fact, I thought to myself, he would probably look even more gorgeous in the Aston Martin V-12 Virage, if that was even possible.

"Let's get the Baroness' account first, and then I will take you for a test drive."

I could hear the excitement in his voice, but the mere mention of the Baroness gave me sourness in the pit of my stomach.

"Do me a favor and let's not talk about the Baroness any more tonight, okay?" I asked.

"You got it, Beautiful," he obliged. "So, where may I have the pleasure of taking you tonight?" he asked with an implied grin on his face. I looked over at his handsome profile lit by the soft blue-green glow of the dashboard lights. There was something sexy about the warm interior glow of his sports coupe. Anticipation hung heavy in the air like anomalous vapors on a lake. Sheepishly I peered over to take a longer look and my heart nearly skipped a beat. I was enamored with his compelling presence sitting there in the driver's seat, poised like a model with his hands on the steering wheel. He had the face of Adonis and I was in his car about to have him drive me home. I wanted him more than anything. I wanted to shamelessly throw myself at him with unchecked passion but I decided I had better cool my jets. After all, he was my boss and besides, there was the whole Baroness incident weighing heavily on my mind.

I looked away briefly to gather my composure and although it was rather dark in the car, I thought I saw a twinkle in his eye as he maneuvered the car out onto the main boulevard. His demeanor lifted my spirits and the excitement of being alone with him, if only for a ride home, began to rise up from deep within me.

"You may *drive* me to my place in upper East Side Manhattan, 88th and 2nd," I said nervously laughing to hide my glee. Patrick gave me one of his huge warm smiles that can melt even the coldest iceberg, and it made me realize that there was no other place I would rather be right now than here, next to my heartthrob.

Traffic wasn't bad for a Wednesday night. We spent the drive chatting lightly about what shows were currently playing on Broadway and which one was our favorite. Before I knew it, we had arrived in front of my apartment. I was feeling so comfortable in his company that I balked at the idea of being all by myself in a quiet apartment. Andrea, my roommate, was out of town this week and I had no desire to be alone tonight. There was an available parking spot on the street and Patrick piloted his sleek Jag into the space like Mario Andretti.

"Let me walk you to the door", he offered clearly noticing my hesitation to get out of the car. He tilted his head down to get a better look at my face, as I lingered in the luxury of my seat.

"Chloe?" his voice was inquisitive and concerned and I felt he could read me like a book. I didn't want to reveal any of the internal turmoil that I was feeling from the restroom event with the Baroness. I was trying to keep it together, desperately wanting Patrick to see me as a strong confident woman, not an Insecure wilting flower. A wave of emotions was building up inside of me and my greatest fear was, that if unleashed, it would knock him over, wash him away and drown our chance at a relationship. *Crap!* Now is not the time to be weak and have an emotional melt down. A guy like Patrick doesn't want a drama queen.

"No, it's okay..." I tried to interject but he was already out of the car and in one smooth move my side door was opened, his hand gracefully extended, inviting me to hold on while I stepped out of the car. He slipped one arm around my waist smiling down at me with that delectable smile of his, charm oozing from every pore of his well-built frame. I wondered if my sigh was audible as I melted into his body, our two forms, making one unified movement towards the entrance to the apartment building. Maybe it was his presence in the immediate aftermath of the harsh events of the evening, or maybe I was just ready for a guy like Patrick in my life. It was a bewilderment to me and I was completely mesmerized by all things Patrick! All I knew was that I felt safe and protected with him and I didn't want to let that feeling go at the door.

We paused at the entryway and he turned to face me with both arms wrapped loosely around my waist. Our eyes locked on each other and I could smell his intoxicating scent.

"Chloe, I'm glad you came by the restaurant tonight." His voice softened.

"I really wanted to see you.... I mean, see you outside of the office. Watching you at work, your beautiful smile, your luscious lips.... It's driving me crazy!" he revealed with a tortured voice.

His gaze was overwhelming and I had to break the intensity for a moment. I tipped my head down to stare at his chest and gently fondled the lapel of his suit jacket between my thumb and forefinger. I was woozy with delight and the excitement of his confession made me rock back on my heels.

Proper decorum dictated that he should let me go inside and the ladylike voice in my head was saying, just let the night end here, but the pounding of my heartbeat was drowning out that voice. Gripped with a mixture of wanton desire for Patrick and sheer dread of being alone with my thoughts for a sleepless night, I lingered longer at the door. His steel-blue eyes were burning holes through me. I was helpless at his command. With one arm he pulled me closer and the other hand lifted my chin with his fingers. My head tilted back in a subservient manner, my lips parted slightly and he gently placed his lips on my mouth.

Slowly guiding his tongue into my mouth he cupped my face with both hands now, passionately and seductively drinking in my kisses, thirsting for more. I gave in completely and threw my arms around his neck, pressing my breasts against his chest and running one hand up the back of his neck into his hair. His last kiss sucked on my lower lip as he pulled back breathlessly.

"Chloe, you drive me wild! You're so beautiful. I want you. Damn baby...." he trailed off as if he wanted to say more. He took one step back and held me at arm's length and scrutinized my entire body then sucked in a breath between his teeth.

"I had better go before I forget that I'm a gentleman..." he whimpered.

As he backed up, I refused to let go and kept the connection with one hand. I desperately wanted him to stay. He gave a little squeeze of my hand that sent my adrenalin pumping. Human psychology is an interesting subject and it is amazing how subtle communication can be. Subconsciously I took his little squeeze as a signal. *Green light means go.*

"Wait. Patrick. Um - don't go." The words spilled out before I could stop them. "Come inside. I don't want to be alone tonight." I pulled him in a little with the one hand, placing the other hand on his forearm and our eyes locked searching deep into each other's soul. I didn't want to seem desperate but I just couldn't let him go. I wanted him and I wanted to please him. In an instant he responded.

He grabbed me by the waist, lifted me off my feet and whirled me around in a circle. We both laughed and noisily entered the building clambering up the stairs, intermittently kissing and murmuring little "m-m-m" noises, as we made our way to my door. We were so hot for each other that the cool night air seemed to sizzle like butter thrown into a hot frying pan, as it crept up the stairwell with us.

My door seemed an eternity away, when I finally fell with my back up against it to search for my keys. He couldn't contain himself and pressed up against me with heated kisses, his hand groping for the hem of my skirt. I finally released the lock and we both rolled in the apartment panting with desire for each other. I flung my keys and purse to the side, not minding that I had missed the kitchen table completely. Patrick spun me around and walked me backwards into the living room area, peeling my coat down off my body in one magnificent swoop, kissing me all the while, unable to take his lips off me.

I fell back onto the couch breathless and panting, as he hovered over me in the soft glow of the small desk lamp I always leave on for safety. He looked magnificent standing there his eyes blazing with desire. He took a moment to let the tension between us simmer and he let his eyes languish a gaze over my body. He slowly took off his suit jacket and laid it over the back of a nearby chair and seductively pulled off his tie, our eyes still locked in a wanting stare. One at a time he popped each button of his shirt in the most sublime manner I've ever seen, revealing a fine taught chest, his tan skin shining in the low glow of the lamp. The view of his bare skin heightened the tension between us even more. His sensual strip tease sent surges of sexual energy racing through my body. I was practically drooling.

Each layer of clothing that was removed added fire to my anticipation of feeling his bare skin next to mine. I ached for his touch. My heart raced and he aroused me to wetness. I sat up on the edge of the couch my face level with his waistline, spreading my legs apart in a tantalizing invitation. I could sense the heat emanating from his body and I inhaled his aromatic spice.

My thong had been torn by the Baroness' angry gesture and there was hardly any fabric to shield the elixir of my wetness wafting up to his nostrils. I struggled to keep from reaching out to touch him, but I wanted to let him come to me. I needed confirmation that he wanted me. Looking down with a fiery smile on his face he accepted my offer and obediently stepped into the space between my legs. Gently reaching down with one hand he began caressing my hair. I couldn't stop the next shiver that flashed down my spine as my blood blazed a trail down to my inner thighs. I craved his body, my entire being aching to please this magnificent specimen of a man.

Pressing my lips to his smooth body, I kissed his rock hard abs, rubbing my hands up and down his backside. With his hands swirling in my hair I looked up, my eyes filled with longing unbuckling his belt and unzipping his pants. As his pants fell open, my eyes delighted in the sight of his muscles, cut in a sexy V shape on his abdomen, the cut lines leading down into his low rise briefs where his hard cock raged against its confinement. Bewitched by his well-defined shape, I was compelled to run my fingers in each groove and depression created by his tight muscles, giving little licks and kisses as I went. Throwing his head back with a long breath he moaned, "Yes, oh Baby, yes!"

There was the "green light" and instinctively I remembered the fantasy I had entertained earlier that evening while masturbating in the restroom stall, so I whisked his shorts down with one hand and wrapped my other hand around his hard manhood. With his hands on each side of my head he purposefully guided me as I took his large cock into my mouth. I worked him over, licking and sucking, letting the whole of his penis into my mouth as much as possible so my hands were free to finish pulling his clothes to the floor. He moaned with ecstatic pleasure with his hands still on my head working it up and down on his cock, until he couldn't wait any longer to have his turn at me.

"Sweet Jesus! You are magnificent, but don't make me come yet, Babe." Lowering himself down to my level on the couch, his hands trailing down my head to my shoulders, he knelt down in front of me between my legs. Working his way down from the crown of my head with little kisses, first on my forehead, then on my cheekbone, he gently traced the very tip of his tongue across the skin of my cheek until he reached my mouth and lapped up my lips thrusting his tongue in my mouth.

The room was spinning, and my heart was pounding out of my chest with anticipation. He kissed his way down my neck to my shoulders, like a kid licking up a river of melted ice cream from an ice-cream cone on a hot summer's day. He unbuttoned my sweater with one hand, pushing the sweater off my shoulders with the other. Magnetic tingles raced all over my body like a network of electrical signals, crossing, connecting and crashing into each other until the infusion propelled a massive rush of exotic energy down to my womanhood.

Before I knew it, clothes were strewn all over the floor and we were naked on the couch, lost in a fervid mashing of bodies. The pilgrimage of kisses continued down my length, his one hand reaching for my clit while his tongue sucked and teased at my nipples. His only respite was to stop for a breath to say, "My beautiful Chloe. You taste like sweet honey"

I was raw with desire. Like the waves of the ocean rolling over me, my passion for Patrick swelled and crashed, the heat of the moment sweeping me under with unbidden ordain.

"Oh Patrick" I moaned arching my back. I spread my legs open begging for him to take me as he adeptly found my clit, swollen and engorged. He sucked in a short breath as his fingers slipped easily around the pink lips of my slit, rubbing with a tantalizing rapid curvaceous motion.

"Oh Baby, you are so wet!" he panted with lavish desire.

I reveled in the excited at the image of him enjoying my pussy and I yearned to satisfy his manly hunger. His hard cock was sharply erect. The sight of it with that blue vein pulsating, straining for release, drove me wild with excitement and my rapture was uncontainable. I desperately wanted to feel the girth of him inside me. I reached out to stroke his penis and in a hoarse whisper commanded, "I want you in me!"

He thrust himself straight inside me, my labia slippery and swollen. He grabbed my hips with both hands, and drove his cock deep into the recesses of my pelvis. He groaned a magnificent sound, confirmation to my ears that I was fulfilling his needs. He rocked his hips, thrusting and positioning me so the head of his penis stroked the G-spot on the upper inside, his gyrations intensifying with every probe.

Just when I could feel he was about to burst, he pulled himself out and flipped me over. With one arm around my waist he lifted me up and bent me over the cushioned arm of the couch positioned to take me from behind. It took me by surprise but *Oh my god,* I loved it. Gripping his massive manhood in one hand he impaled me with his penis, his other hand smacking my butt cheek with a sharp whack.

As he was deep inside of me, I could feel his body up against my backside. Reaching his free hand around to my mouth, he traced his fingers over my lips. I willingly kissed his fingers and sucked them like it was his cock.

His hand fondled my clit again as the raking of his cock against my hot spot and the fast pulsating motion of his fingers, moved me to the brink of orgasm. He blew out his breath in gasping unshackled pants on my back as he raged inside me and stroked my pussy.

The intensity of my sensations brought me to the edge of the cliff, one more stroke and he would send me over in an explosion.

With one final tug of my clit, he pushed a momentous stroke and roared, "You're all mine!" as his cum filled my already dripping opening and I went sailing over the proverbial edge into ecstatic oblivion.

*I was hooked!*

# CHAPTER 6

The sharp sun glared directly into my eyes. Throwing my bent arm up over my face to shield them, I stretched my body to its full length.

*Shit! I forgot to close the blinds last night.... LAST NIGHT!! OMG!!!*

Memories of the previous night's events came rushing into my mind, and in a quick motion I flipped over in my bed for a reality check. There he was right next to me, sleeping like a baby.

*Wow! Even in the morning he looks like a Goddamn movie star!*

The alarm clock flashed 6:05 AM. Still another twenty-five minutes until it would ring. I quietly slipped out of the bed trying not to wake him.

As I stood up, my head felt like a broken down pinball machine that had "TILT" written all over it. I stumbled into the bathroom, opened the cabinet door searching for those Advil I knew I had somewhere.

*Found them! Hmm, only two left.*

As I made a mental note to buy more Advil, I

washed down the two pills with lukewarm tap water. I brushed my teeth and began removing my make-up from last night. One look in the mirror told me I looked like a dirty dish rag and I was in need of some serious touch-ups. I couldn't let him see me like this, but luckily; I still had some time before the sound of the alarm would wake him.

I tiptoed to my vanity table, routinely applying my three-part makeup ritual as best I could despite the jack-hammering going on in my head. *Argh! Puffy eyes! I'm never drinking again!* What made me think drinking was a good idea in a situation like last night?

With exactly four minutes before the buzzer would kick in, I snuck back into bed, trying like James Bond to stealthily maneuver my way under the covers, with as little movement as possible.

"Good morning gorgeous", Patrick said softly into my ear as he wrapped his arms around me. Voluntarily, I snuggled my body next to his, enjoying the curvilinear design of our intertwined bodies.

"Morning handsome," I smiled back at him rolling my body to face his, our foreheads touching. He traced his fingers gently along my jawline and gave me a little kiss on my nose and I was beaming. *I could get used to waking up to this every day!*

"I hope I didn't make a fool of myself last night. Um...a little too much for me to drink...I think..."

"You - are nothing but sweetness. Don't worry about it. We've all done that once in our lives," he murmured.

The comfort in his voice released my unfounded anxiety and my spirits soared. I was on cloud nine and blissfully wiggled in a little closer.

The alarm buzzer rang out a stark reminder of my obligations of the day but my heart fluttered at the thought of spending another work day in the presence of Patrick Collins.

Playfully smacking his hand on my butt cheek he chided, "Come on sleepy head, we're burning daylight!" Jumping out of bed, he bent down and brushed his lips to my forehead, then jaunted out of the bedroom in search of his clothing strewn about the living room.

Slipping on my pink robe, I sauntered out to purvey the aftermath of last night's sexcapades on the couch. My gaze fell on Patrick standing at the door all dressed in his suit and ready to go, twirling my thong panties up in the air on one finger, like he was sporting a well-deserved victory trophy.

*Shit!*

My eyes zoomed in on the lace edging that was ripped off in the brutal attack, my anxiety magnifying degree of the tear a thousand times over. Did he see the damage? Did he notice? I couldn't bear to tell him what had happened and I promised myself I never would. I tried to make light of it all with an offhand remark.

"Um, looks like a bomb went off in here!" I said with a nervous laugh attempting to play it off.

"There were some - *explosions*- in here last night,

well, several explosions," he teased.

I blushed a little at his play on words.

"Guess I don't know my own strength!" he continued as he examined the thong.

*Damn! He noticed.* I wanted to get those underwear away from him tute suite, so I continued my bleak attempt at a diversion and quipped back, "Yea. More like - earthquakes. Earthquakes and explosions!" I bargained.

I feigned a laugh and rolled my eyes at my own immature humor. I lurched forward trying to snag the panties from his grip, but he just raised them up higher teasingly out of my reach. Each time I would lunge forward he deflected my advance, twisting so they would be just out of my reach. He held them up high enough so he could give me little pecks-of-a-kiss each time I jumped for them. He was so tall and handsome I forgot in an instant what I was reaching for. Finally, he let me win the silly game and allowing me to snatch the panties away.

In a huff I said, "Those will be going in the trash now," and I crumpled them up in one hand. I buried them in the kitchen trash can, pushing them far down into the can as if the act itself would hide the dirty little secret which they held.

As I returned to the living room, Patrick was fishing his necktie out of the prawns of the fake potted palm near the door. He turned to me and said, "If you have plans for Friday, cancel them. You are coming with me to an art showing."

I blinked in bewilderment, my mind racing through my schedule.

Friday? Friday?

What was I doing Friday? *Wait! I don't care what I am doing Friday. I want to be with Patrick.*

My confusion obviously showed on my face and he furrowed his brow for a moment, as he opened the door to leave. He paused in the door frame and grinned saying, "A good of friend of mine is having an exhibit. I'll pick you up." With his hand on the door knob poised to pull it shut, he leaned in and gave me one last quick kiss on the lips. "Be ready at seven..." And I stood there bemused, staring at the closed apartment door, Cirque du Soleil doing flips in my stomach wondering, "What have I gotten myself into?"

I turned around and the panoramic scene of the living room, with clothes still flung recklessly about, met my eyes. As I began cleaning up, picking up my sweater, skirt and shoes, I reached for my purse, perched askew on the edge of the table and fished out my cell phone. *Shit!* It's probably dead. In my fervent hunger-lust for Patrick I had forgotten to put it on the charger.

*OMG!* Five missed calls and a gazillion texts from Elyse! I scrolled up the missed calls list and hit the reply button for Elyse, bracing myself for what would come next.

"My God Chloe, are you alive? Where've you

been?" My friend shot out a rapid fire hail of questions. "Can't you send a girl a text?"

"I'm sorry. I know. I know. I'm bad." I was dying to tell all.

"I was sooo bad... And it was sooo good!" I played with the words to heighten her curiosity even more. She didn't need to put the screws to my thumbs. I sang like a choirboy, spilling my guts about the previous night's events, my voice squeaking with excitement as I gleefully divulged the delights of Patrick. A glance at the clock and I realized I still had to shower and get ready for work and much to Elyse's chagrin, I had to cut her short. She pressed me for all the dirt, but I just couldn't bring myself to reveal the horrid details of the dark washroom incident with the Baroness. So I begged off with the excuse that I had to catch the bus soon and ended the call.

I literally twirled and danced my way into the shower to get ready, girlish giggles bubbling up to my lips; a silly tune playing in my head to the beat of the "conga line" song, "I-got-Pat-rick-Col-ins. I-got-Pat-rick-Col-ins."

I mused at how I would nonchalantly saunter into the office today, keeping a poker face in front of the gawking office hens who would be hulking over me like vultures, and waiting for some tell-tale sign of happiness or joy. Some of my female co-workers were ruthless gossips seeking to live vicariously through the escapades of others. It gave me a creepy voyeuristic feeling, being someone else's entertainment. They must like to watch. *Yuk!*

But truth be told, my mind was twisting and turning with more important things. There would be various scenarios I would have to encounter while working with Patrick in the office. How was I going to handle it? *Cool as a cucumber Chloe, cool as a cucumber.* I couldn't allow my actions to reveal the steeping sexual tension building up between us.

*Argh! Sleeping with the boss Chloe, sleeping with the boss!*

My mother's voice was chirping in my head. I wrinkled my forehead into a frown. That voice was always such a killjoy. Where's the mute button for the mother voice when you need it?

Dreamy sweet Patrick! My heartbeat quickened every time I thought of his kisses and now, after a night in his arms, I had more fuel to the fire my steamy daydreams of surrender. Surely I would be a mess at work until the art exhibit on Friday.

# CHAPTER 7

"Liz, I need a huge favor. Can you help me?" I whimpered.

Elyse looked up from her desk with curiousness and surprise.

"Why are you still here Chloe? Don't you have an art exhibit to get ready for?"

"I do, I do, but that stupid jerk Jeff from the accounting manager's office, who obviously hates me, just ordered me to type up twenty pages of notes and he wants them today!" I exclaimed desperately. I was holding out the stack of papers that he had just handed me, giving Elyse the most begging facial expression that I could possibly manage.

"Any chance you could..." I pleaded.

"Give me those papers you little crybaby," Elyse offered.

"Thank you sweetie, thank you sooooo much", I uttered delightfully and quickly forked over the papers before she could have a change of heart.

"Yea, yea. You owe me one, Chloe," she yelled as I

dashed out towards the elevators.

I ran to the curb to hail a cab. No bus tonight for me. I was a woman on a mission and I had to hightail it home to get gorgeous for my hunk, Patrick. The day had passed tortuously slowly, watching the clock and counting down, first the hours, then the minutes, until finally, I could turn my thoughts with abandon, to being with Patrick, the handsome, rich and successful fine specimen of man!

The anticipation of the night's events to come sent my blood rushing through my veins. Adrenalin flooding my central nervous system made my stomach feels like it had been left on the highest crest of the roller coaster at Magic Mountain. My nerves popped like firecrackers, as random memories of our erotic night together created a sentient mosaic in my mind. His lips, his deep set eyes, his curly dark hair, his gentle touch, his....man parts! *Whew! Mamma mia!* What was I going to do with this man? And what about that ink stain, the Baroness?

*Piss on her! Tonight I'm gonna par-tay!!*

As soon as the cab reached my place, I shifted into high gear and dashed up to my apartment. Luckily, I had already planned what to wear the night before so I wouldn't waste time getting dressed. I'd put together a hot, sexy outfit with a short black skirt, knee high spike heeled black boots, and a two layered black top with peek-a-boo fabric that allowed the under layer to be seen through the sheer top layer. The bottom layer covered everything necessary, but the sheer fabric on top allowed just enough light through it to see the skin beneath. I accentuated the black top with some shiny silver jewelry, nothing too trendy, something with a little sophistication; after all, I was going to an art exhibit in New York City.

I made my eyes up in smoky shades of blue gray. My eyes were one of my best feature, or so I'd been told, green, with little flecks of brown. Bending over at the waist I brushed my hair upside down to give it some lift. I was lucky to have long straight hair that usually cooperated into whatever style went with my outfit. Tonight I decided to leave it loose and flowing, so that it would swish in a tantalizing way for Patrick to see as I walk across the room, a prompt eliciting ideas of what he could do with me later.

Tonight would be a test. I wanted to see if this would develop into something serious, or if a fun office affair was all he desired? Had I correctly read the messages in his eyes when we made love?

The muscles in my stomach contracted and rolled in response to the thought of him thrusting hard inside me. I wiggled a little as I sat on my make-up stool pressing my legs together to hold that delicious urge for later.

I had just put the final touches on my ensemble when I heard the lobby buzzer. He was downstairs. My blood pressure spiked and I blew out a short breath in an attempt to relieve my nerves. I was as skittish as a cat on a hot tin roof. I buzzed him up and in an instant he was smiling at me in my doorway.

"Come in" I said breathlessly. "I hope I look okay? I'm not over dressed for this, am I?"

"Yes, way overdressed," he teased. "Hmm. Let's see."

Lifting the tip of my scarf between his forefinger and thumb, he gave a long languid look down my body and holding the end of the scarf up he said, "Everything but this..... Take it all off. Naked and a scarf will do!" he smirked with a grin and gave me a soft sweet kiss on the lips.

"Seriously, you look divine and just as beautiful as always Chloe!"

Placing his hands on my arms, he pulled me into his chest where I could smell his wonderful delicious man smells. I reeled, weak in the knees, so many bees buzzing around inside my head, a momentary lapse of consciousness and spontaneously my head fell back a little and my lips parted. I opened my eyes to his intense, burning stare; those eyes, those steel-blue eyes, windows to the soul, wreaking havoc on my psyche.

Cupping my face in both of his hands, he poured his passion on my mouth with unchaste desire. My lips vibrating with nerve pulsations, I met his advances, returning his kisses with matched intensity. Tugging, teasing, sucking, our rhythms matching, we danced this heady dance for what seemed like an eternity. Like a rock skipping across the surface of a pond, a thought came glancing across my subconscious. We had an event to attend and placing the palms of my hands on his chest I coyly pushed back, putting a little space between us.

"Down boy!" I said playfully. "If we continue like this we'll never make it to your friend's gallery."

"You are just so delicious. I can't keep my hands off of you." he murmured running the back of his hand down my cheek.

Grabbing my coat, he whirled me away to his sporty Jag which he had parked on the street, floors below. It was uncanny how this guy had a knack for catching a parking space.

As we drove to the art gallery we chatted lightly about art and the various galleries in the city. I couldn't help but stare at his dashing profile. I cocked my head to one side and a little forward in order to study his expressions as he talked. It occurred to me that this might be a good time to question him about his past. After all, I really didn't know much about him. I knew he was confident, persistent, a hard-charger, but what about his past? I did know that he graduated from Columbia University but I mused, does he have his success today because of a well-connected family? Or did he work against all odds to climb his way to the top? I liked the later of two scenarios. I preferred to think of him as a self-made man and not the recipient of favors owed to his father.

And what about his private life; his love life? He's 38, not married, has a sister and niece, but no kids of his own and no girlfriend, or any such relationship of which I am aware. *Humph!* I snorted. *No relationship that I know of.* Everyone has skeletons in their closets. Before our conversation allowed a proper opening for my questions, we had arrived at the art gallery. A little disappointed that I missed my opportunity to know more about Patrick, I was bolstered by the chance to finally meet someone who had known him for years. Patrick had told me that the gallery was one of several that his lifelong friend, Ryan Barrick, had started. Tonight, I wanted to pick Ryan's brain for any insights into the mysterious background of Patrick Collins.

We parked the car, and he came around to open the door extending his hand the ever gentleman. The automatic reaction was a telltale sign of good manners instilled by his upbringing.

"You look good stepping out of a Jaguar Miss Swanson. It suits you well." he said in a low voice pulling me close as I stepped out so his lips brushed my ear and I melted a little on the inside.

Patrick had told me on the way over that there would be light hors-d'oeuvres at the showing tonight and I assumed there would also be spirits of some sort, to loosen the tongues of all whom I would blithely interrogate, Patrick to be included. And with a quick kiss on the lips he ushered me into the red brick building on the lower east side of the city.

The minute we walked through the doors I was taken aback at the sight that unfolded before my eyes. I paused in my tracks.... "Whoa!"

Patrick chuckled at my reactions and playfully jested, "Oh, did I forget to mention that this is an erotic art showing?"

"Yeeaa... you forgot to mention that detail!" I retorted with a pitch in my voice that made yea a two-syllable word and taking my hand he pulled me out of my bewilderment.

"Come on," he chuckled. "You must meet Ryan. We knew each other in college you know."

"Of course. Columbia, correct?" I replied. *Ah, an opening. Let the inquisition begin.*

"Ryan started out as a business major, like me, well, marketing through a business major. He's a great guy, very creative and inspirational."

"I see." I said capriciously, as he guided me around a three foot sculpture of an erect penis, sitting on a pedestal, strategically located in the foot path to the interior chambers. The sculpture was massive, dark green and poised, like a rocket, ready to launch into a tunnel made of coiled barbed wire. Needless to say, an erotic art show was a new experience for me and the irony of it all gave fertile ground to the many jokes and puns sprouting in my mind.

At the next turn of the gallery hall, I was affronted with a twelve foot high, oils on canvas; a painting of a singular erect "Penis with balls", as it was so aptly titled. My curiosity was piqued. Oh, and women, in the most unusual poses, bodies, contorted into shapes that I didn't even think humanly possible.

"Tell me more," I dubiously asked cocking my head to one side as we passed another large painting on a canvas. I didn't want to stare, but I found this genre of art interesting and yet frightening at the same time. Patrick chuckled and pulled forward on my hand. I was relieved that he didn't appear interested in lingering to purvey the paintings at any length.

"Don't worry, Baby, not all of Ryan's galleries are like this one. He has others with, well, shall we say, more refinement and elegance. Ah, here we are," he said as we came upon the hors d'oeuvres and drinks. He took control, ordering me a drink from the beverage bar.

"A drink for the lady please, make it champagne." He turned and smiled at me. I answered with lifted eyebrows and a mock smile that said *la-ti-da! I could get used to this kind of treatment.*

Patrick passed me a glass and was about to take his when a voice rang out from the group behind us.

"Hey, Patrick ole' buddy!"

In an instant, he whirled around with a big smile on his face and yelled, "Ryan!"

A slender, dark-haired trendy looking man embraced Patrick, the two of them doing the guy hug thing, slapping each other on the back. It wasn't hard to see they were good friends from way back.

"Good to see you Ry" Patrick said and I watched his face fill with enjoyment.

"Ryan, I would like you to meet my friend, and lovely assistant, Chloe." His eyes twinkled. Ryan smiled a warm smile and shook my hand.

"It's always a pleasure to meet a friend of Patrick's, Chloe." I blushed a little at all the sudden attention on me, but mostly at the comment from Patrick.

"I do hope you are enjoying the erotic exhibit. It can be a bit unnerving if you have never been to this type of art show, I must say," he conceded.

"I have to admit it was a little startling when I walked through the door. Patrick didn't tell me what kind of show we would be attending, just said it was an art showing," I laughed in acknowledgement.

"Hey now," Patrick said with playful hurt in his voice.

"Maybe he was hoping you might get some ideas once you saw the art!" Ryan interjected with a laugh.

I blushed a little again.

"You should see his other galleries Chloe; someday I will take you to all of them." His eyes beamed down at me stirring a little flutter in my stomach. *Hmmm. Someday?* Does that hint at a future for our relationship?

"How do you two know each other?" I quipped. "Did you grow up together?"

"Ryan and I met in college, at Columbia. Originally, he was majoring in business like me but after college, he changed directions."

"That's right," Ryan commented. "I worked in the

corporate world for a while but it just didn't satisfy me, it wasn't my thing. One day I met this young artist, you know, the kind that's magnificently talented but unfortunately, his artwork wasn't getting noticed. I rented a small space in Manhattan and turned it into an art gallery. Thanks to my friend's talent and maybe a little luck, my gallery took off. "

I could see the pride on Patrick's face at his friend's business acuity for launching such a risky endeavor. Patrick had to jump in and finish the story for Ryan.

"Since the first one did so well, my boy Ryan here bought another one and then another one and the rest is history!" he said with a clap on the back, Ryan grinning at his friend's complement.

"Patrick, my dear friend," Ryan said, "It's great to see you. I'm so glad you came tonight but I'm afraid I must go mingle and take care of the evening's business." Turning towards me with smiling eyes, Ryan addressed me.

"We don't want the guests to start copulating in the gallery!" he said smiling with raised eyebrows. "I hope you two are staying for a while."

"Of course, Ryan," Patrick replied and with that said, Ryan bowed out through the small group of people huddling near the bar area.

Patrick turned his full attention on me with a big smile. "He's amazing. I can't tell you how much I love that guy. The good times we had in college....well, you don't want to hear about that now, but suffice it to say, he's a funny guy and a smart businessman too. What he did with that first gallery of his...... you'd be blown away....."

"Yea, he seems like a really nice guy," I added.

His excitement settled a bit and his focus changed. He looked deep into my eyes as I stood there sipping my champagne. He moved a little closer to me those steel-blue eyes so inviting. I could see that he truly was excited to reconnect with his old friend but I had discovered very little about his past from Ryan. Oh Patrick Collins! Your true inner child continues to elude me! All I knew was that the champagne was going to my head and I was standing in the middle of a room, surrounded by eroticism with Patrick's breath in my ear.

With one arm around my waist and a glass of champagne in the other, he nuzzled my head, his breath ruffling whips of my hair, breathing in the scent of my hair and perfume. The rush of blood in my veins temporarily muted the sounds in the room and my awareness of time and space dropped off the grid for a brief moment. It happened once before, in the conference room, when he leaned in to talk in my ear and I heard nothing but white noise rushing in my ears. It's as if our physical bodies took a timeout turning all communications over to our souls, letting them have their own magical way of communicating. No one had ever had this effect on me before.

As quickly as it came, the moment left me, and I

could hear his words in my ear, "Baby, you smell heavenly. I could just eat you up tonight." He tried to look like he was just talking in my ear, but he gave a nip at my earlobe before he pulled back with a devilish smile on his face.

Teasingly, I bit the rim of the champagne glass with my teeth, peering up at him from under my lashes.

"Want some dessert?"

"Well, that depends. What's on the menu?" he said with a low seductive voice, his eyes burning through me. He took a quick glance around the room and then his eyes focused on a door with a small staircase to the second level.

"Come. Let's check out the rest of the gallery." A seductive grin was plastered on his face. He reached over to the bar taking a drink and handed me a fresh glass of champagne and took one for himself. With his free hand he took mine and lead me across the room to the small staircase chatting as we walked.

"This space was such a good deal for Ryan. He always manages to get the best deal for the price."

He led the way up the stairs. I expected the upper level to be spacious but I was surprised to find a dead end, except for one door to each side of the landing..

"I wonder what's in here?" he hesitated. "Maybe just storage space. Let's check it out."

As Patrick pulled the door handle, the door sprung open. Smiling a thief's grin he motioned with his arm for me to enter first.

"Are you sure we are supposed to be up here?" I was feeling a little uncomfortable nosing around Ryan's gallery.

"Ah, it's Ryan's office," he realized as we stepped inside. I surveyed the office for a brief moment, after Patrick clicked on a small desk lamp that created a yellow glow to the room. He set his drink on a heavy dark mahogany desk that had a glass top layer over the wood. It was the typical office set up, a computer on the desk, a phone, file cabinet and a small settee at one end of the room. I followed him as he wandered over to look at a memorabilia wall at the end of the office.

"And that's me right there! See?" Patrick was pointing towards a large photograph hanging on the end wall. As we stood there examining the photo, he gently pulled us closer and I noticed it was a picture of a much younger Patrick standing with an equally young Ryan, in what looked like a college dorm room.

"This was taken by Ryan's dad when we were freshmen, the day we moved into our room at Barringer Hall."

I sensed a touch of nostalgia in his voice. It felt so comfortable standing next to Patrick with his arm around me. Smiling, I rested my head on his masculine chest,

"Awe, you guys looks so cute and handsome together." I teased.

"Ha, ha! Don't tell Ryan that. We don't want him to get wrong ideas in his head," Patrick said with a wink.

He turned to face me and smoothed a few fly away strands of my hair back into place that got messed up from having my head on his chest. I volleyed back one more time in our game of conversational quips.

"Oh, you mean he's gay?" I said bluntly, but not completely surprised.

"Well, let's put it this way," he said with a purr in his voice. "I have never heard him brag about doing this to a girl!" He cupped my face in both hands and slowly, teasingly ran the tip of his tongue around my lips before passionately plunging it into my mouth. The familiar rush of blood ran its course through my veins and I felt my body heat spike to a roaring fire. Our tongues danced a fiery dance in our mouths, and I felt an urgent surge of desire when his tongue swiftly glanced the edges of my teeth in the sexiest move I had ever experience. He gently and slowly walked me backwards towards the desk.

*Oh God this was delectable!*

The thought of sex in a public place triggered a frantic lust in me that I had never experienced before. The taboo was just more kindling to the pyre and my breath hitched with excitement. Patrick was commanding the moves and this was totally hot!

Astutely guiding me, he moved me in the direction he wanted by pressing his body, hands and lips towards his target. Tugging at the hem of my skirt, roving up and down my body, frantically pushing and squeezing at my breast; his hands found my clothing an annoying tactile barrier.

As we moved past the door towards the desk, he reached over and clicked the lock with one quick flip of the wrist and continued the assault with his tongue in my mouth, stopping me just at the edge of it. I was breathlessly panting and my body ached for his touch. He paused for a moment to drink in the image of me wanting him, his steel-blue eyes piercing and raging with purpose. The introspection was so intense I parted my lips with a small gasp, "Oh Patrick." I swooned. He licked his lower lip and placed both hands on the bare skin of my outer thighs slowly pushing my skirt up around my waist.

I planted my butt cheeks on the glass of the desk and leaned back supporting myself with my arms behind me. I moaned and arched out to meet his advancing kisses making my legs as straight as possible while still on the edge of the desk. Smoothly and gracefully he kneeled down in betwixt my legs, his fingers tracing around the edges of my thong panties. As he began kissing my upper thighs I felt the softness of his lips and the warmth of his breath feathering across the epidermis. The anticipation mixed with the thrill of getting caught made for a heady cocktail in my body.

*Oh God Patrick! Just do it!*

Holding my panties in one hand he slipped a finger under the edge of my string bikini and pulled it aside, revealing my bare mound. I moaned with anticipation.

"Mmmm, this is a lovely dessert!" he crooned. I

stiffened my legs even more thrusting my private parts in his face in a "*just take it*" message. I couldn't wait much longer; I urgently needed his touch. As if to read my mind he ran his finger around the outside lips of my slit, content with the wetness he had created. He sucked in a breath and in a husky voice said, "Ooh baby, look how wet you are for me."

I moaned and arched again. Holding the panties aside, he spread the lips of my pussy apart to expose my tingling clit, engorged and pink, standing at attention from the raging hormones in my body. In one magnificent gesture he drew my wetness up from within me to moisten my clitoris. The feel of the moisture hitting my clit sent me to a new level of ecstasy. I longed to scream out in pleasure but knew I had to stifle my intonations for fear of someone hearing us. The frustration just added to the rapture of the situation.

He only gave me one little taste of pleasure and then spreading my labia wider he blew gently on my clit. A heavenly sensation flooded my brain. My awareness of the room was fading, the familiar rush of the white noise filled my ears again making the thrust of his fingers inside me an erotic surprise as he pressed his mouth directly on my pulsing clit, licking and sucking with hot nasty vigor.

" I think we need a little flavor" Patrick teased and he dipped his finger into the glass of champagne next to me, letting the bubbly liquid drizzle over my slit, lapping up the delicate sparkling drops with oh so much finesse.

"Oh fuck, Patrick! That's so good!" I felt the muscles tighten deep within my loins, my heart rushing the blood in my body to the critical accumulation point, putting me at the brink of orgasm. His rhythm quickened, his two fingers stroking the upper inside of me, hitting my g-spot with a little "come hither" motion and his tongue flicking and swirling, building up a delirious storm. I was floating on the edge, my body wound tight, begging for release and with one hard press of his tongue; I sailed over the invisible edge into ecstasy, and shattered into a million pieces.

I leaned forward, waiting for my breathing to still, my wrist aching from holding my weight to the edge of the desk. Patrick came up to meet me with an affectionate kiss on the lips. With his hands on my waist he pulled me off the desk to stand before him but this time I took control. I took his hands off me and placed them at his sides. I put my hands on his waist and moved him back a step giving me some space to kneel down in front of him.

We locked gazes, no words needing to be spoken, all intentions screaming out in the vibrations of our bodies. My hands started unbuckling his belt and I made my way down to the floor. Involuntarily his hands went to my long loose flowing hair and he gurgled in a husky voice, "Oh Baby!"

His cock was straining in his pants and he gazed

down at me with abundant accommodation, the ever present frenzied fear of discovery, weighing on my mind. I worked quickly at releasing his massive cock from his drawers, smooth, pink, and protruding, begging to fuck my mouth. Obligingly I grasped his throbbing erection with one hand and clasped my lips around its expansion. He threw his head back with a hiss of pleasure. I purposefully stroked him, sucked him and worked my tongue around the head of his penis.

He swole in proportion to my measure and gently moved my head in accordance to his thrust. As he swelled, I cupped his balls in one hand squeezing them up with enough force to create an erotic blood rush, forcing his ejaculation. Groaning from between his clenched teeth, I felt his warm salty release fill my mouth and slide down my throat the only place it could go without leaving evidence.

*Damn!!* The sharp jiggle of a door knob straining the lock, hit my ears like a bullet out of a gun. *What the fuck!*

"Aw, man, what timing." Patrick only seemed mildly annoyed at the intrusion on our tryst. It was quite obvious that he was not as bothered by the danger of our secret escapades as I was. I had the "deer in the headlights" look about me and Patrick just chuckled. He took my hands and helped me to my feet then buckled up his pants.

"Chloe, your emotions are so fresh," he said softly, holding my chin in his hand.

"You are so hot! And, that was literally mind blowing!" he remarked referring to my handiwork. I smiled and felt the heat rising to my cheeks.

"I think we should get out of here before they come back," I said nervously biting my lip. I pawed through my hair, using my hand like a makeshift comb. It had been messed up by Patrick's love dynamics. He noticed my gesticulations and helped me smooth my hair with a little chuckle.

"Here, let me," he said and sweetly caressed my hair in place and then gave me a kiss on the nose. I straighten my skirt and realized that I needed to use the restroom after all that champagne.

"Wait, where's my purse?" I asked looking around the room. We both turned at the same time to look on the desk where my purse lay sprawled next to my drink glass. "Oh my God," I gasped. Simultaneously, our eyes caught sight of a large smudge left on the glass desk top, a residual impression of my butt, clearly created by the sweat of our steamy sexcapades!

"Wipe it off, wipe it off!" I begged clutching my purse to my chest and holding onto Patrick's arm.

"No, let's leave it as a little souvenir for Ryan!," Patrick answered with a boyish smile. "It is clearly the nicest piece of erotic artwork I have seen tonight!"

Playfully punching a clenched fist at his upper arm, I loudly objected, "Stop it now! Let's go find the restroom."

"It's right across the hallway I think." Unlocking the

door, Patrick took my hand, sheepishly peering out, to see if the coast was clear and ushered me out to the small area at the top of the stairs.

"I'll wait for you here," he said courteously as he opened the bathroom door for me. I ran a comb through my hair and reapplied my lip gloss as I laughed to myself, *"Who knew art showings could be so much fun?* Just as I was about to toss the paper towel in the trash, I heard a soft tap on the door and flung the door wide to Patrick's smiling face.

"Beautiful as ever!" he beamed, his eyes bright and glossy. He offered me his arm and escorted me down the stairs to the gallery area below. When we entered the gallery again, I dipped my head down to my chest a little, as I was sure my face would betray me. Thankfully, most of the people had their eyes fixed on the pieces of art and not on me, though now, ironically, after just having sex upstairs in the office, I *was* one of the erotic artworks!

"Before we leave I just gotta say goodbye to Ryan," Patrick insisted and no sooner had the words come out of his mouth when a familiar voice resonated in my ears.

"There you are, Patrick." Ryan's voice chimed out. The direction of our bodies responded like a tracking device and turning around, my eyes fixed on an edgy looking guy standing next to Ryan.

"Patrick, Chloe, I have someone I'd like you to meet. This is Vladimir. He's the genius behind all these amazing pieces." Ryan went through all the formalities as he introduced us to the artist.

"Pleasure to meet you Madame," Vladimir replied with a thick eastern European accent, as he pressed his lips to my hand with a slight bend at the waist.

*"Good thing I got a chance to wash my hands before meeting this guy!"*

Driven by the memory of our upstairs adventure from a few minutes earlier, I struggled to suppress the chuckle threatening to erupt inside me, .

"Vladimir is from the Czech Republic," he continued. "We met last year when I was traveling in Europe. He is the reason I decided to open a gallery focusing only on erotic art. Don't you think his work is absolutely stunning?"

The pitch in Ryan's voice rose increasingly higher as his excitement mounted, while he described a very detailed anecdote in which he found this street artist having breakfast in a small town cafe in Prague.

Glancing at his watch, Patrick finally broke in, grabbing Vladimir's hand in a fast pump handshake.

"Well, it's been really exciting to meet you Vladimir. Best of luck with the exhibit. I'm sure there will be lots of takers for these exquisite pieces. Unfortunately, Chloe and I have to dash off so we don't lose our reservations at China Grill," he apologized.

"Always good to see you buddy!" Ryan responded with sincerity and gave Patrick a warm hug.

"Chloe, an absolute pleasure to finally meet you, but

be careful with this guy," he said pointing his chin at Patrick. "I've heard he has a few tricks up his sleeve, ha ha!" A warm genuine smile broke over Ryan's round face as he leaned in to give me a sweet kiss on the cheek.

"Nice to meet you too," I confessed. I genuinely liked Ryan and was pleased that I had finally met someone from Patrick's past, giving me a small window into his personality.

# CHAPTER 8

The evening was progressing splendidly, and I stepped lightly as Patrick escorted me to the parking garage behind the gallery.

"China Grill?" I asked curiously.

"Yes, I made reservations there in case you might be hungry. What do you think?"

"Sure! I would love to. I've heard it's really nice".

'The food is out of this world. You'll love it"

A few minutes later we were cruising down Fifth Avenue in his sporty Jag towards the fabulous China Grill.

*What a wonderful night this is! I hope it never ends!*

I felt light hearted, carefree and all the sensations of the spring season were upon me. I opened the window a crack to let in the cool night air. The breeze felt refreshing as it blew my long hair in whips around my face. I looked at Patrick sitting next to me with his face upturned, feeling content in his presence.

"Ryan is a really great guy. Did you know he was gay when you shared a dorm room?" I asked quizzically.

"Truth be told, no! But I had my suspicions. We never really talked about it but I always wondered why he never hooked up with any girls when we went out. Honestly, I thought he was just a bit shy." He snickered, giving me a broad smile.

Patrick maneuvered the car up to the valet curb, shifted into park, leaned over and gave me a sweet little kiss. My limbs felt light as a feather and If I had checked in the mirror, I'm sure my face would be glowing.

"Let's go eat. That finger food concoction at Ryan's gallery wasn't enough to fill a grown man's stomach," he said as the valet opened my door.

"Welcome back, Mr. Collins."

We were greeted by a beautiful, dark-eyed, slender built Asian. Patrick must dine here regularly, I mused, considering the fact that as soon as we walked in he was greeted by name by this exquisite Asian hostess.

"Right this way, Mr. Collins," she said with a seductive smile. "Your usual table is ready for you."

"Thank you Mai," he coolly answered back his expression unreadable.

"Come here often?" I asked with a little edge to my voice and stoically walked towards the table. The green-eyed monster had raised its ugly head and I was annoyed by this woman. With such a starkly good looking man on my arm I would have to get used to this kind of reaction. *Guess I had better step up my game.*

"Not as often as I would like to I'm afraid. The food here is excellent. Have you ever eaten here before?"

"No, this is my first time. Can't really afford these kind of places with my salary you know" I said shyly.

"Ahh, we will have to do something about that. You wait and see," he said as he valiantly pulled out my chair.

Patrick ordered champagne and we leaned in, toasting to an incredible night. As we talked for what seemed like hours, his fingers absentmindedly stroked the handle of the silverware, first the fork and then the knife. I shook away the image of those fingers running along my skin instead. Sipping, and chatting I was lost in his eyes and the world soon fell away.

Before I knew it the table was filled with plates of various delicious Asian delicacies.

"We will just share everything. That way we can try more items. I'm sure you will like it," he suggested."

The words were barely audible to my ears as I was swept away by my imagination. In my eyes Patrick was perfect. And so was this dinner in this upscale restaurant, where the food was just as amazing as this hot and sexy man sitting right in front of me.

Reaching his hand across the table for mine, and gazing deeply into my eyes, he said, "Chloe, tonight has been wonderful and I don't want it to end. Let me take you to breakfast."

"But it's ten o'clock at night." I was momentarily perplexed at his remark.

"Exactly" Patrick's eyes bemused me and I blushed. My heart hungered to spend the night wrapped in his strong comforting arms. I didn't want the magic to end either. *Ever!!*

He drew my hand to his lips and kissed my fingertips. Mouthing the words against my skin, I could feel the movements when he said, "I have never met anyone like you Chloe. You are beautiful, strong, and confident and I can't get enough of you."

My heart melted, I felt the butterflies kick up in my stomach and a shiver of excitement ran down my spine. This was what I wanted. This is what I had hoped my destiny would deliver to me, a handsome, rich, single, ever attentive man like Patrick Collins. Everything was moving along smoothly like skating on a sheet of glass.

After the lavish meal, we drove to his Manhattan penthouse apartment, Patrick playing soft smooth music in the Jag and me floating on cloud nine, my head filled with a soft hum of knowing exactly where I wanted to be in my life. Just when I thought things couldn't get any better, we arrived at his place and I was like Cinderella at the ball. The opulence of the building left me gaping. Soon after parking and going through a series of security passes, I stepped over the threshold into his apartment and couldn't help but take a step back, gasping as my eyes scanned the open white space like a radar detector.

"Oh Patrick. This is magnificent!"

I couldn't help but feel like a little kid in a candy

store my neck craning side to side like watching a tennis match, as I took in every detail of the modern clean living space. The floors were light Beech wood, and everything else, the walls, ceiling and lamp shades was snow. Snow with one exception, the outside wall of the building was glass, top to bottom, with nothing but beams of brushed stainless steel where absolutely necessary for support of the building, beautifully framing the Manhattan skyline.

Patrick's taste is furniture was exquisite, modern, sleek, and minimalistic with bright accents of red used sparingly. The living room had a large white leather sectional couch with a graceful curve at one end and smooth round edges. Who knew there could be so many shades of white? It was marshmallow on snow. The lights of the city flickered and blinked through the massive window wall. If the windows could be something in nature, they would be crystal. I dubbed this room as marshmallow and crystal on snow.

Patrick took my coat and laid it over a chair.

"Welcome to my humble home," he said graciously as he walked to touch a rocker wall switch. A white sphere of a lamp shade that hung down from the ceiling lit brightly then dimmed to an ethereal glow as he slid the gradient switch. Once the lighting in the room was to his liking he motioned for me to sit

"Please Chloe, have a seat. I will be back in a minute," he said touching his lips to my forehead and dashed into the other room removing his suit jacket as he walked.

With great delight I chose to park my behind on the luxurious white couch. It felt smooth as kid leather. I couldn't help but rub my hands over the surface as I sat waiting for him to return, petting it like a kitten. I was feeling warm and fuzzy inside, little waves of anticipation forming in my nervous system, a pleasant shudder going through my body. I leaned back, stretching my legs out a little when a provocative thought popped into my head. A little smile spread over my lips and I closed my eyes, as I pondered the idea of having marshmallow sex on this beautiful couch. It was a little unnerving when Patrick popped back into the room at the apex of my thoughts. *I swear, he's freakin-psychic!*

"Is everything okay, Chloe?" His eyes were warm and sea-watery blue as he gazed down at me on his couch.

"I love this place Patrick! A girl could get used to this," I teased as he sat down beside me on the couch his lips brushing my temple.

"You are sweet." He nuzzled my hair with his nose leaning in to inhale my scent, his breath ruffling whips of my hair..

He nipped at my ear and stroked my locks with his hand. I rolled my head into and out of his nuzzle in an obliging fashion, feeling the familiar warmth of my blood smoldering within my veins.

"Come on. Let me show you around," he murmured.

Standing up he took my hands to help me to my feet, then lead me down an appropriately white, long curved hallway, to his white-infused master bedroom. As I approached his chambers I heard the mesmerizing rise and fall of instrumental music.

Upon entering the room I was transported by the color scheme; white and its soul mate, without question, black! My eyes drifted for a moment to the walls, decorated with stylish black-and-white photos of Paris, but the ambient glow of a fireplace, soon drew my attention.

*Oh baby!* The image of Patrick in front of a fire, with the glimmer of the fireplace lights bouncing off his bare chest, tooled up my already fevered blood temperature another hundred degrees.

"Patrick, you never cease to amaze me," I asserted as I spied two wine glasses sitting on a chic art deco coffee table in front of the lapping flames of the fire.

"I want to pamper you Baby," he said as he stroked my cheek with the back of his hand down to my chin. Slowly he placed his lips on mine in one salacious preview kiss, pregnant with the promise of more. My heartbeat accelerated and my breath was escaping in small pants. He paused a moment and I could see the desire burning in his eyes.

"Do you even know how much you tempt me every day with your seductive eyes?" he said in a low sexy voice and gave me directions with a nod towards the couch. With my feet barely touching the floor, I glided over to the small sofa in front of the coffee table and fell into the seat like a cog in a wheel. I took off my boots and got comfortable in front of the fire shadows, dancing on the white walls behind me. Patrick scooped up a bottle of Pinot Grigio from the wet bar and joined me in my reclining seated position, kicking off his shoes before he sat down. He poured some wine and placed the bottle in a chrome wine bucket.

In the past week I had pictured myself straddling him on a desk, fantasized about him to the tune of my own touch in a restroom stall, witnessed his release at my apartment, painted an erotic scene with him at an art gallery and now, the transcendental atmosphere of Patrick's bedroom was replete with copious memories of a lifetime. He poured us each a glass of white wine and leaned in, his glass poised in midair, waiting for my glass to mate with his for a "cheers-clink".

"Here's to tonight. Cheers, Baby." Our glasses kissed and we sipped. The wine slid down my throat with ease, like hard butter on a hot knife warming me from head to toe. I flushed. I moistened my lips and looked up from under my lashes gazing into Patrick's eyes. He was so good looking it took my breath away. It should be illegal to be that handsome and unattached. I twitched in my seat, pressing my legs together, feeling like my wetness was rubbing off on the rich leather of his love seat.

"To us" I said, "And whatever tomorrow may bring."

A precursory smile spread across my face, as the effects of the wine shifted me into low gear. The rush of the alcohol into my blood washed over me like a languid wave. I began to feel lightheaded and carefree, losing all inhibitions but the salacious mood of the evening threatened to loosen my lips. I was afraid I would pour out all the things I wanted to say to Patrick. I wanted to tell him how completely he affected me that he drove *me* crazy too. And if I wasn't careful I would let him drive me, like his Jag, anywhere he wanted to go. He had an enigmatic power over me that spurred my inner voice to caution. But I wasn't listening to that voice tonight I wanted to be with him without limits.

We drank a while on the couch in front of the fireplace and then in an amazingly hot move, he pushed the table aside and pulled me down onto the rug in front of the fireplace, placating me with fiery kisses all the way to the floor. He laid me down like a present on Christmas morning and slowly began to un-wrap me.

Lying on the rug to my side he draped his fit upper body over mine; kissing my neck, while working the top button loose. As he worked his way down, he laid open the fabric exposing my bra and heaving breasts, giving equal attention with his lips to each creamy white crest. His hand smoothed and swirled over my breasts, pushing and squeezing, tugging at my bra, aching for the touch of my flesh. I closed my eyes to accelerate the intensity of my other senses to his caresses. The touch of his hands, the fire of his kisses, blurred all of my senses into one sizzling concoction of surrender.

Deliciously delightful sensations raced through my body a hundred miles per hour, careening down to my inner thighs and sex, lighting it up like a Christmas tree. In the blink of an eye he shifted positions, moving to sit back on his heels at my feet so he could peel my skirt off, panties and all, wriggling it over my hips and down my thighs. I sat up shrugging my blouse off my shoulders and he threw off his metallic grey shirt with the flair of a magician's cape. The highly sculptured surface of his chest was further defined in the glow of the fire. My movements betrayed me and I licked my lips panting with desire.

I ran my hands up his thighs as he stood before me, his diamond cutter bulging within his pants. Kneeling down in front of me he took my face in both hands, running his fingers up through my hair, and directing the full brunt of his passion at me, he ravaged my mouth with his supercharged tongue, kisses spilling over me like fine wine. His desire for me was insatiable. He couldn't stop touching me and I didn't want him to stop, as my lust was equally matched to his desire.

He moaned and bristled with need.

"Let me fuck you from behind Baby," he growled and turning me around he steered me to a new position, pulling my knees up under me. I heard the familiar zing of his zipper and I knew he was out of his clothes like a pedal to the metal.

Both hands slid up over my butt cheeks to my lower back and all the way up to my shoulders, pushing my hair to the side, then back down again to my ass. Swirling one hand over the roundness of my cheek he sucked in a breath between clenched teeth, hissing with approval. He used one hand to spread me apart while palpating the viscosity of my wetness with agile fingers of the other.

"Oh Baby. All wet and ready for me," he breathed in a low husky voice.

He fondled my slit and tweaked my clit, thrusting two fingers inside of me in a precursory gesture. I arched and moaned, voraciously wanting more, his tactile swirling and rubbing, coaxing me into a pyretic frenzy of desire. Skillfully he orchestrated my orgasm tenaciously crafting my rise towards ecstasy when, the next thing I knew, he had me, all four on the floor, mounting me from the rear, sliding his cock down into me. The long slow slide in, sent a responsive moan to my lips. Each stroke stretched me, the friction signaling a cavalcade of new erotic sensation to my brain.

Holding the curves of my hips, he stroked me from behind, smoothing the cheeks of my elevated ass with the palms of his hands, alternating gripping my hips for the up thrust and shifting too low for the down stroke. His body bent over mine, staccato breaths powdering my back, he growled like an unleashed beast.

Like a piston in a crank shaft, he pumped me hard. I

could feel the muscular tone of his thighs, slamming up against the back of my upper legs, vibratory jolts cascading throughout my entire body domino style. His steady pumping picked up speed, ramping me up and just when I felt like I would spin out of control, he reached around and in one touch of my clit, pressed my magic button, holding it firmly in place. Controlling my revolutions per minute, he let me idle, stalling me, in a deliberate orchestration of my release. He pulled out and rolled me over onto my back.

Panting and wanting I laid there wondering why the hell he had stopped! Gracefully and athletically he carried me over and gently laid me on the bed. He climbed on board, and spread my legs open with his knee as he positioned himself kneeling over me, his raging erection beckoning for me to suck it. I reached out with one hand and stroked its magnificent length, running my hands down around his balls, squeezing and pushing them up a little. He moaned and looked down at me, fire blazing in his eyes, his one hand fondling my moistness and the other assisting me with my piston-like movements on his cock.

"Not so fast Baby. Let's take our time to enjoy this."

"Mm-m-m, I am," I purred. I had never had a man control my pleasure like this before. The building up and waiting and building up again was intoxicating. Most of the guys I had known, where the "Wham bang thank you ma'am" type, interested in their pleasure, not mine. *This was pure heaven!!*

He leaned over to the nightstand next to the bed and picked up a small bottle. Straddling one of my legs he poured some oil from the bottle into his hands. The aroma of the oil filled the air as he smoothed and swirled the oil across my breast, stopping to pinch up each nipple as his hand passed it. He massaged my breasts and stomach making curvilinear lines as his hand worked its way down my stomach to my abdomen, pausing frequently to give little kisses to my breasts and belly. The combination of warmth and fragrance was hypnotic. The progression was a familiar one, breasts, stomach abdomen and .. and.... I shivered in expectation.

*Oh please, touch it!* The tension inside my body began winding up like a tightly sprung coil, as the anticipation of feeling his hand on my clit started my engine again. And in an effort to rev me up even more, he slid his hand past my hot spot, onto my inner thighs, oiling and lubricating each one in turn. My entire body tingled with excitement. I couldn't hold still. I wiggled my hips and stiffened my legs. He grabbed both my wrists at once and pushed my arms up over my head.

"No, no, not yet, my pet," he crooned in a low voice.

Holding my arms in place with one hand he kissed my neck, and then sucked my nipples, right and left and then on his hands and knees reached again for the night stand.

"Hold still and close your pretty little eyes. Just focus on the sensations," he murmured.

I willingly obliged his every command. I felt the warm pressure of the palm of his hand as it passed over my abdomen, thighs and my bare mound. Filled with sensual satisfaction, my body thanked him with an involuntary moan and arch. I felt one hand placed flat on my mound and then the cool sensation of ice, first on the outer edges of my pussy and then straight down the center line, moistness rolling down my lady parts, from the application of the ice to my hot skin, the combination of hot and cold, arousing whimpered little "ooos" and "mmmms" as he passed the ice between my folds. On the last pass of the ice, as it was melting down to practically nothing, he held it yo my clit, spread me open and put his mouth right on it, ice and all, sucking both clit and ice into his mouth, continuing the onslaught of my senses with his tongue. My eyes popped open, I moaned with delight and rolled my head to the side thrusting my hips, I offered up my taste for his erotic pleasure.

His tongue flicked and lapped, swirled and sucked and the spring coiled tighter. My breath was escaping in pants, the tension was rising, and I could feel my muscles tighten. All my blood rushed to the the magic spot and with his fingers inside me and his tongue working its magic, the sky fell and I was stolen. I came, jetting wetness into his mouth and I let out a triumphant groan, *"Oh Jesus muther-fuckin Christ!!!"*

My arms came down from above my head as I raised up and I gripped his wrist hard, digging my nails into his skin. Panting, he grabbed at the wetness with his tongue.

"You tastes so good, Baby," he rasped and I fell back completed and spent.

He rose up to his knees gripping his erection, ready to fill me with his manhood, eyes ablaze and evidence of his wanton desire oozing from the head of his penis. The sight of him there hovering over me, hard cock in hand, escalated my need to feel him inside of me. I thought of him in my mouth, then I thought of him inside and opted for the later knowing the deep satisfaction I would feel from him coming in me.

As I reached out to touch him, he read my mind and thrust his fullness in my slit guiding it in like holding a saber. The pleasure sensation of stretching skin sent white lighting to my brain and I reveled in it. I wanted him to spill his seed in the deepest part of me, as deep as any human could ever be with another person, setting the foundation of life's most eternal bond. He gasped and groaned with pleasure letting his body come down on top of mine. I could feel the rock hard muscles of his bare chest on my skin and his heavy breathing in my ear. I pulled my legs up, knees to chest position, to give him an even deeper thrust. Together we kissed, and panted, our bodies writhing with pleasure as he cranked up his rhythm and went at me full throttle. I clutched the muscles of the walls of my vagina around his cock inside of me. With one last forceful thrust into my depths, he shuddered and I felt his release. Satisfied at last, his body relaxed and he shifted the mass of his weight to the side to so I could breath. We laid there, waiting for our breath to slow, wrapped in the warm afterglow of mind blowing sex.

He pulled me in snuggling his body next to mine nestling his head in the area between my chin and shoulder. He inhaled, quenching his thirst for my scent and in a soft voice said, "You are truly divine, Miss Swanson. Intoxicating... like a fiery shot of Patron."

His compliments made me blush a little and I said, "Well, Patrick, you are pretty amazing yourself." I wasn't about to let him know that he was the first to ever touch me that way and that I had never allowed myself to feel such heated passion before.

He lifted a strand of my brown hair and sifted it through his fingers as if he was thinking of the right words to say. Traced his finger down my cheek he lifted his head, giving me a gentle little kiss on the lips.

"Well, my dear, I'm every bit of smitten with you," he whispered. "Now, if I'm going to treat you to breakfast, you should get some sleep. You've had a long day... work, an art showing, and now, hours of exhilarating, orgasmic pleasure..."

"Mmm Patrick," I warbled. "I guess you just bring out the best in me!" Teasing him with a smile, I playfully delivered a gentle smack on his muscular biceps. I felt so very connected to him, like I had known him my whole life, his energy strangely familiar.

"Sweet dreams Baby," he said and wiggled in a little closer.

"Sweet dreams," I said and closed my eyes hoping to extend this otherworldly feeling and continue my adventures with Patrick in the etheric universe of dreams.

# CHAPTER 9

The next morning, my olfactory senses woke me with a barrage from the rich aroma of freshly brewed coffee mingled with crisply fried bacon. Looking down at the sheet pulled up over my breasts, I remembered the events of the night before and a pleasant grin spread across my face. I rolled over and stretched like a cat. Looking around the room that was flooded by the morning light, I inhaled deeply and thought, *DAAAMMM! He cooks too!*

I jumped up, throwing on his shirt that was lying near the couch from the night before, as a makeshift robe. After a quick pit stop in the bathroom, I padded down the hall to the kitchen to see Patrick making an omelet. He had obviously gotten up before me and was dressed in low-rise, True Religion jeans and a tight, black, V-neck-shirt. Two place settings with coffee mugs were set out on the black granite countertop island bar.

"Good morning sleepy head." Patrick beamed and came over to give me a little kiss.

"Good morning" I chimed in.

"Did you sleep well?" He continued talking and pouring coffee.

"Yes, delightfully well," I confirmed and put my head down a little, reminiscing about the events of the night before.

"Cream and sugar?" He asked, more as a confirmation than a question, as he poured me a cup.

"How do you know?"

"I've seen you take it that way at the office," he chuckled. "We *do* work together you know." he said with a big smile.

I rolled my eyes with a little "aw shucks" kind of look, but I was impressed that he had paid attention to such specific details about my wants and needs..

"That looks great," I said pointing to his omelet pan on the stove, and I took a seat at a bar stool with the coffee he had prepared for me, just the way I liked it. With a mock southern accent I said, "Why Mr. Collins, I do declare! I didn't know you were a man of so many skills!" and batted my eyes like a southern Belle. He shook his head at my bad acting and served us breakfast at the kitchen island.

We chatted lightly, joking and poking fun at each other's regimented work habits, when we were interrupted by the universal ping of an iPhone text alert. We both startled a little, craning to hear whose phone gave out the sound. It was Patricks' and flicking the screen with his thumb he opened the text. I took the opportunity to clear the dishes, while he read the text, and then sat down next to him.

"Well, there's a turn of events," he said putting his cell phone down on the counter. He sat with one foot propped up on the rung of the stool and one hand resting on his thigh.

"What's that?" I inquired.

"My niece. She's gonna bail on me." He chuckled and shook his head in mock disbelief. "She can't make the charity event in the Hampton's next weekend. You know, the one I had you buy the dress for."

"Oh, really? That's too bad. It was such a nice dress," I offered. "I can't believe she wouldn't want to be with her favorite uncle," I said as he pulled me in front of him. Slipping his arms around my waist, I stood eye level to him..

"Yea. Imagine that! She would rather go to London with her mom." He feigned hurt. "But seriously, my sister is a journalist and has an assignment in London so, she's taking CeCe with her as a birthday gift. Guess I've been kicked to the curb."

He wiggled me side to side with his arms around my waist, lights sparkling in his eyes.

"Tell you what. Since I no longer have a date, Chloe, I would love to have the honor of your beautiful presence with me at the charity event in the Hamptons."

My eyes widened and I swallowed hard.

"I'd love to!!" I squealed in a voice sounding like Mickey Mouse. I was practically jumping up and down.

"Ahh, what will I wear? I don't have that kind of dress, or the money...."

"Don't worry, Sweetie. You already have a dress and one you picked out yourself!"

With a look of discernment on his face, Patrick jumped up and exited to his bedroom before I could protest.

"No really," I yelled down the hall to him, "I couldn't. It wasn't meant for me..." but my words fell on deaf ears. I bit my lip with a mixture of angst and excitement.

In a flash, Patrick came out holding the black gown I had purchased just a few days ago. The beauty of the dress still took me aback. I stepped forward to stroke the fabric between my fingertips and although a part of me knew I should say no, something inside me was pleading to say yes.

"Oh, Patrick. I can't...."

"Of course you can." He said definitively. "You know you look smashing in this dress.

"But..but.."

"I'm not taking no for an answer. It's a done deal. You're going with me, in this dress and you're gonna be a knockout." He leaned over and gave me a peck on the forehead and I rolled my eyes like a reluctantly compliant child.

I looked at the time on the microwave clock and mentally checked my schedule for the day. I had promised Carly, my roommate that I would pick her up at the airport. She was due back after a week's visit with her parents. I couldn't wait to tell her the news. I was going to *the* premier charity event of the summer, in the Hamptons, with the incredibly handsome and successful, Patrick Collins. A farm girl from Iowa couldn't ask for more!

# CHAPTER 10

I had just checked my hair and makeup for the nth time in the last hour when I heard the buzzing of my cell phone on the table. Instinctively, I grabbed it.

*Another message from Patrick:*

"On my way. Be ready in five."

I was already packed; in fact, I had been waiting for almost an hour. It was Saturday past noon and he was late but that was okay. After all, no one wants to be the first to show up to a party. I wasn't sure what to bring and had packed way too many outfits, but then, I'm like that, I can't decide until I'm in the moment, what will strike my fancy.

*Hope my two bags will fit in the trunk of his Jag.* I ran a hand through my hair. My mind was already on the road when suddenly, I heard the now familiar sequence of five distinct knocks on the door.

"Coming," I called out with excitement. I quickly unhooked the chain and opened the door with a big swoosh. A huge warm smile greeted me when our eyes met and Patrick immediately picked me up in a big bear hug, planting a long hot kiss on my lips.

"Hey Baby, so sorry I'm late. I had to go into the office and attend to a couple of issues. Are you ready?"

"Yes, I hope you have room for my stuff in your little sports car," I said waving my hand towards my luggage.

"Wow! You know, we'll only be in the Hamptons for the weekend," he said surprised as he eyed two large, bright red suitcases.

"But I can't decide what to wear. It might be chilly there and I have to bring matching shoes for each outfit." I whined a feeble explanation, desperation clearly showing on my face.

He gave me a bearing smile and grabbed the two suitcases.

"Geez, What did you pack in these? Bricks??" he mockingly grunted, struggling somewhat to maneuver the two large suitcases towards the door.

"No, silly, I had to make sure to bring enough suntan lotion for your pale butt cheeks," I laughed as I slapped his firm behind. "We don't want them to get burned!"

He gave me a wink as the elevator arrived and down we went to his car. Ten minutes later we were cruising on Freeway 678 towards Route 27, which would take us all the way to the Hamptons.

"We should get there in about two hours," he said nonchalantly tapping his thumb against the steering wheel as he drove.

"Perfect! I love road trips. Where are we staying, by

the way?" I queried.

"I booked a cottage for us. It's a very nice little inn. I've stayed there a couple of times before. It's in East Hamptons and brags of being very romantic."

"Sounds wonderful. I'm so excited. Our first road trip," I said with a big smile trying to hide the cloudy thought that just crept into my mind. *Hmm, very romantic place...* I wondered how many girls he'd brought there before me. Oh well, the past is the past. I brushed the thought away like dust in the wind. We all have skeletons in our closet, and I'm sure that with Patrick's good looks and fine physique, he's had more flings than most guys.

"I was thinking; let's have an early dinner at the inn. They have a Scandinavian salmon on the menu that is to die for. It's called Gravlax which is a cured salmon. It's delicious!"

"Quite frankly, I am starving," I said. "Can't we just pull over for a Big Mac instead?"

Patrick gave me one of those, *"Are you kidding me?"* kind of looks and I couldn't help but burst into laughter.

"I'm joking, Babe. Everything sounds wonderful and you are wonderful," I said leaning my head onto his broad shoulder as the scenery flipped by us like pages of a book.

I inhaled his scent; a slightly sweet, but fresh cologne. It was intoxicating. Every moment with Patrick made me feel wonderful. He was perfect and so was this trip. Slowly, I slid my hand over, resting it in his lap when I suddenly felt a small reaction rising up from inside his pants.

"Ooh, what do we have here?" I snickered, teasingly rubbing my hand against his inner thigh and crotch.

Startled, Patrick recoiled with a jump, glancing over at me with a lighthearted glint in his eyes. "Careful baby, let's make sure we get to the Hamptons in one piece."

"If we pull over for a moment I will show you how much I appreciate you inviting me here this weekend," I said enchantingly.

Patrick hissed a breath through his clenched teeth, "Oh baby, that's a very tempting offer and extremely hard to resist. There's nothing that I'd rather do, but hold that thought for later."

"Awe!" I mockingly stuck out my lower lip and pouted.

"Besides, I have a surprise for you. Our cottage has a luxurious private spa and I know a trick or two when it comes to giving a sensual, bubbly massage."

I pulled my hand back from his crotch and gave him the, "I'll behave for now" look.

"But let's keep moving, okay? he suggested. We're already a little behind schedule."

As we drove along Route 27 I turned and looked out the window. The scenery had changed. We were getting closer to our destination when I was reminded of something that Patrick had once told me; that the

Baroness owned one of the largest mansions here in the Hamptons. As my mind wandered, I speculated about what had ever happened with her and the retail account? *Did our agency get the bid?* Secretly, I hoped not. That woman gave me the chills. Actually, it would be no sweat of my back if I never saw that bitch again.

As if Patrick could read my mind he suddenly blurted out, "Oh, by the way, guess who sent me an email this morning?"

"Who?" I tried to sound perky.

"The Baroness, Anna Von Lamberg. She wants to move forward with the account if a couple of conditions could be met. That's why I had to go into the office before I picked you up. I had to revise the proposal. She'll be at the event tonight."

My heart fell out of my chest like a bomb had been dropped. *Damn! I really hoped she was history.* Crestfallen, I turned my head and looked out the window so Patrick couldn't see the bitter disappointment on my face.

"Are you okay?" he probed.

Doing my best to hide my utter distaste for the Baroness, I looked him in the eyes and proclaimed with a frown, "I'm fine. It's just that.... I' m getting a strange vibe from that woman. I'm not sure she likes me very much."

"Don't worry so much about that. I already told you, that she can be peculiar and demanding. She's so egotistical that she treats most people like dirt. She'll warm up to you eventually I'm sure." He shifted his driving position, placing both of his hands on the steering wheel in a manner that seemed to punctuate his sentence.

*Crap!* I nodded in implied agreement, knowing in my heart that it would be a cold day in hell before that would ever happen.

# CHAPTER 11

"Chloe!" A familiar voice rang out in my ears. I turned and saw Ryan striding towards me in the main foyer of the Crestwood mansion in the Hamptons.

"What a breath of fresh air it is to see you my darling, in this over pretentious crowd," he proclaimed.

My eyes lit up with surprise. "Ryan! So good to see you too.

I didn't know you would be here tonight, I thought Patrick was bringing his niece, but I'm so glad you are here," he continued.

"And...may I add, you look stunning!! Oh My God! That dress suits you to a T!"

"Awe, thank you Ryan" I said demurely.

"Are you as bored as I am?" he grinned. "Where

have you stashed my buddy? You know, you two really make a nice couple."

My heart lightened with the thought that Patrick's best friend, not only approved of us, but referenced us as "a couple".

"He's around," I said sweeping my drink glass in a half circle to my right. "He's talking and hobnobbing with the VIPs and, to answer your question, yes, these people are rather dull. But I don't mind, this mansion is gorgeous and I'm thrilled to be here to support the charity. Patrick said he'd be back in a few minutes. He had some business to discuss with Mr. Graywell from the Betsey Johnson account."

"I love Betsey Johnson designs; you should be in that meeting with him. I'm sure you know more about Betsey Johnson than he does."

"It was more about some contractual issues, not like a creative meeting," I added.

"Are you sure he's not in search of some glass topped desk," he chided with a smile.

"Oh my God, you noticed?" The thought of Patrick's friend touching my ass print on his glass desk made me red with embarrassment.

"Yea, like a kid with his hand in the proverbial cookie jar," he laughed. " I had to invest heavily in Windex just to get it clean! It nearly broke my heart to erase such a great work of art!!" He smiled back at me.

"Err, sorry about messing up your office Ryan," I added, "I don't know what's come over me lately. It seems that Patrick has a hypnotic effect on me. Normally, I wouldn't do never do that, but hey, you only live once....." I giggled. The bubbles of my peach Bellini were having their way with my inhibitions once again.

An astute waiter appeared at my elbow holding a tray with a small cream colored envelope on it.

"Excuse me Miss. Are you Chloe Swanson?" he asked with perfect enunciation.

"Yes, I am." I perked up. What could this be? Does this have anything to do with Patrick? The waiter handed me the envelope and turning on his heels, floated off ubiquitously, into the mix of people. Ryan's eyebrows raised and I had a funny feeling that I shouldn't read this in front of anyone.

"Excuse me Ryan," I said politely and stepped over to a small ante room near the entryway. My nerves began to jitter like a box of Mexican jumping beans. Tentatively, I slipped my finger under the sealed flap and ripped it open. The note inside read:


Chloe,

Meet me in the library in 5 minutes.
I have another little surprise for you.

Anonymous

A huge smile spread across my face. I felt sure that, even though all the people were in the other room, they could see me blushing. Surely, this was Patrick's way of teasing me about the Gallery incident. Apparently Ryan was right about Patrick. He must have been scouting out a new desk top to defile. Giddy as a schoolgirl, I slipped the note into the envelope and headed back to politely excuse myself, but Ryan had been absorbed into the crowd and I couldn't see him anywhere.

Weaving a path through the elegantly dressed couples, a waiter directed me towards the library. I worked my way up the plush red carpeted stairs to the second floor. As I approached, I noticed the dark oak door to the library was opened a crack. The muffled murmur of a male voice was drifting from the room. Was Patrick talking on the phone? Why is he talking to himself? What could it be? My heart was pounding, my mouth felt dry. I practically tip toed up and gently pushed open the door. I could see a familiar figure in the room. Patrick? As the door swung open farther, I recognized the silhouette. It was Patrick but my heart dropped like a bomb to the bottom of my stomach. What I saw made my eyes open wide and my jaw drop in disbelief.

*What the fuck!!* Patrick was in a deep lip lock with none other than the Baroness!! His back was to me and he hadn't seen me enter the room, but as soon as they felt my presence in the room, they broke apart.

"Chloe!" the Baroness said cunningly. I see you got my little note!

"Patrick! What is this?" I said with surprise and hurt in my voice.

Patrick wheeled around and started walking towards me. "Chloe, this is not what it looks like," he stuttered.

The Baroness smoothed her hair back in place like a disheveled teenager in a recent make out session and before Patrick had a chance to say anything further, she cut in, "Chloe, I was trying to tell you all about it last week but you refused to listen. Patrick and I are together again. We have been seeing each other for almost a year now..."

"I...I can't believe you would do this Patrick!!" I said shaking my head in disbelief, fighting back the urge to give in to the tears welling up in my eyes. A huge knot rose up in my throat, choking me and making me sputter out the words.

" Why? WHY?? "

As he sprang towards me with an outstretched arm, in a feeble attempt to explain, I backed up towards the door. My emotions were exploding inside of me like a volcano. My breathing was shallow and I couldn't get enough air in my lungs. I stumbled and backed into the door twisting out of Patrick's outstretched hand, as he was about to grab my arm.

"Chloe. Wait! Let me explain," he pleaded desperately.

I couldn't see clearly through the tears, my mind was whirling with thoughts, the emotions of betrayal and hurt fighting to have their place in my mind. My head was conscious of nothing but feelings and feelings were torment. Encompassed in a luminous cloud of which I was merely the fiery heart, my emotions swung through unthinkable arcs of oscillation, like a pendulum. I had to get out of there, I couldn't breathe. I didn't want to hear some fallacious explanation. I had been used and abused. I knew it all had been too good to be true. A handsome, rich guy like Patrick wouldn't really want me, small town Iowa girl when he could have a Baroness billionaire. Who was I kidding? What a fool I had been!!

*I had been fucking played - big time!!*

All I wanted to do was run away, and run I did. My feet just kept moving, my physical body making decisions for me when my intellect had been effaced. I rushed out of the room unaccompanied by thought. I ran out of the library, down the stairs and straight out the door of the most beautiful mansion in the Hamptons. Before I knew it, I had run all the way down to the beach and the sound of the crashing waves, broke the haze of confusion, which was congesting the thoughts in my mind. My lungs engulfed a great draft of air, which was instantly expelled as a shrieking sob. My chest convulsed and the tears raced down my cheeks.

Just like a cheesy soap opera on reruns, I played

back the scene with Patrick kissing the Baroness over and over again. In an attempt to connect the dots and make sense of it all, I searched the recesses of my mind to find the clues as to why this had happened. Could I have been so oblivious as to have missed important signs that revealed that they were lovers all along? Was I so blinded by my love for Patrick that I made myself vulnerable to the crushing heartache I was now feeling? Could I even blame Patrick for playing the field and looking out for his own interest and the interest of the company?

*Damn right I could!!*

How dare he use me this way! He had no right to play with my emotions, hurting me, like I was merely a chess piece in his slimy scheme to take over the Baroness' account and further his career, at my hearts expense.

Standing knee deep in the murky water of the Atlantic ocean I felt completely numb. I was so desensitized that I couldn't even feel Patrick's hand on my shoulder.

"Chloe, please let me explain," he said in a soft voice.

His words compelled me to turn around, and I could see the desperation and pleading in his eyes. My brain was on fire; my heart, which had been fluttering faintly, gave a great leap, trying to force itself into my throat. My entire body was raked and wrenched with hurt!

"Explain what Patrick? That you used me and

fucked me for pleasure, while at the same time fucking that old hag baroness for money, like a gold digging gigolo. Is that what you are trying to explain to me?" I sputtered with rage. "Just save it Patrick! There is nothing you can say that will rectify what you've done. In fact, how much do I owe you for the privilege of putting your cock in my mouth? Do I have to tip you as well?" I seethed.

Shoving his arm off my shoulder, I scooped up my shoes and headed towards the mansion.

The desperate sound of his voice rang out behind me, "The baroness and I are not together. We were never serious. All we had was a small fling last year that ended shortly after. I did *not* kiss her back today. I was trying to explain to her that I didn't reciprocate her feelings and that we would never be together. She practically jumped me and that's when you walked in. I swear!"

Patrick was now far behind me when I heard him yell, "I even told her that I was in love with someone else. And it's true. I am in love... with you Chloe."

I stopped in my path, turned slowly and looked up to the library balcony. The French doors pushed wide and the gossamer white curtains billowed out the open door. Standing there in the night air with her arms folded across her chest was the Baroness. I saw the eyes of the woman who had destroyed everything, gazing down into my own through the moonlight. They were the eyes of contemptuous satisfaction. I remembered having read that men are hardwired to betray and how easily we can allow ourselves to be deceived by false realities.

And there was Patrick, the man I had fallen in love with, standing at the edge of the sea, his expensive designer shoes buried deep in the sand, salty water undulating around them like a water snake. Looking like a beaten dog, I realized that this was probably the last time my eyes would gaze upon the incomprehensible Patrick Collins.

Over time, we all commit acts with intentions, either good or bad, that require forgiveness and this would take a lot of forgiving.

Nothing left to say for now except.....

*It's over!!*

To be continued in Deceived Part 2 - Paris

# ACKNOWLEDGMENTS

First, I would like to thank all of my readers. Without you, my books would not exist. I truly appreciate each and every one of you. I would also like to give a big "shout out" to the girls in the Smutty Book Whore Mafia on Facebook. You girls rock! Without your connections and support, "Deceived" wouldn't have had such a good beginning. I enjoy the humor and candor with which we interact, not to mention the awesome photos! They give me lots of inspiration for writing my steamy sex scenes. I especially want to thank, Andrea Gregory, Helen Read and Belkis Williams for beta reading Deceived Part 2 and being my biggest supporters.

I would also thank my mentor and good friend Raine Miller for all your help and guidance. You rock!!

A big "thanks" goes out to all my Twitter followers and Facebook friends, all several thousands of you, who keep me tweeting into the wee hours of the night.

Finally, I would like to thank my editor and book cover designer, Primrose Book Editing and Design. Thanks for all of your help and clever ideas.

# ABOUT THE AUTHOR

Eve Carter is a true romantic at heart and with a modern contemporary erotic twist to her romance novels, you had better fasten your seatbelt, as the ride is always fun, exciting and fiery.

Living in Southern California, but a mid-westerner at origin, Eve finds plenty of inspiration for her books in her own exciting life. Eve has always loved the arts and as a young girl, she took dance classes and spent the summers reading books from the local library.

Fascinated with the written word and its power to guide the imagination, Eve started writing short stories and later took Creative Writing classes in college. Eve graduated from The University of Iowa with a B.A. in Journalism and an M.A. in Higher Education. She also has a Teaching Credential from Chapman University in Southern California.